Doubting Thomas

Stephanie Taylor

Clean Reads
www.cleanreads.com

DOUBTING THOMAS
Copyright © 2010, 2017 STEPHANIE TAYLOR
ISBN 978-1-62135-664-6
Cover Art Designed by AM DESIGN STUDIOS

For everyone who ever saw my worth

Chapter One

HER RED HAIR shone like a beacon in the foggy air as Thomas Williams entered the pool hall that night. Shaking his head, he tried to ignore her. It was the same woman who had stared him down the previous night while her boyfriend looked on in obvious confusion. She was alone tonight, but the place was crowded with men who watched her closely. Surely she'd find someone else to annoy. He wasn't interested in whatever game she played.

Yet she continued to stare right at him.

"Iced tea, please," he said to the bartender who gave him a grin.

"I should have known." He handed Thomas the glass. He leaned over the bar and settled on his elbow, cocking his head to the side. "So. That cute little redhead over there has been asking about you."

Thomas almost choked on a swig of tea. "What?"

"She was curious about what happened to you." The bartender glanced up at his face and then looked away, standing erect and vigorously drying a glass with a towel.

"Most people are curious. What did you tell her?" Thomas tried to keep his eyes averted but he could feel the intensity of her stare against his back. By all rights, he should be used to that kind of stare, but something about her made him curious.

"Same thing I tell everyone. To ask you."

Thomas nodded once in gratitude. Two men abandoned a pool table to his left, and he grabbed it. He was almost done loading the rack when he noted, out of the corner of his eye, the redhead moving toward him. He ignored her and leaned down to break.

Thomas scratched the ball when her behind, clad in tight jeans, leaned up against the table so close he could have moved an inch to his left and touched it.

"I hear you're pretty good at pool," she said.

He grunted in response and bent, doing everything he could to ignore that shapely behind, but it was right where he needed to line up his break. He stood and looked at her with a cocked eyebrow, trying to convey his annoyance. It didn't matter that she was the prettiest thing this side of the Mississippi, he didn't want the trouble she was no doubt offering. He ignored the sweet smell drifting to him despite the cigarette smoke and beer. He couldn't quite place it, but it filled him and caused his senses to heighten.

"How did you get that scar?"

Thomas sighed and clenched his eyes closed for a moment. "Why do you want to know?"

She raised a mocking eyebrow in a way that made her look both sexy and cute. "I'm just making small talk."

Her innocence was completely bogus.

"Small talk usually doesn't entail butting into people's business."

"Sore subject?" she asked.

"No, just none of your business."

"So you won't tell me?"

"Where is your boyfriend?" he asked impatiently, looking around. He wanted this woman out of his hair so he didn't do something he would regret. His own temper had a way of getting the best of him when he least expected it. The last thing he wanted to do was scare her.

"I don't have one."

"So the guy you were all over last night isn't a boy-friend?"

She shook her head.

"So, you're a hooker then? You must be getting low on cash to approach me, but I can tell you right now, I've never once had to pay for sex and I don't intend to start now." He was pretty sure that was a true statement. If it wasn't before his accident, it was now.

"I'm not a hooker, I'm just curious."

"Well, don't be."

"My name is Alyssa." She waited expectantly.

When she said nothing else, he offered, "I would say nice to meet you, but I don't really want to encourage you."

She grinned. A cute little grin that made his insides mush. "How about we change that?"

Thomas erected himself and sighed. "Just tell me what you want."

Her gaze slid down his chest, and he could imagine how smooth it would feel if it were her palm instead. He cleared his throat and kept a steady eye on her face.

"Just to talk," she said softly. "What's your name?"

He rolled his eyes and turned to line up his shot, this time pushing past her so she had no choice but to move. She waited until he sank several balls before approaching him again. "Was it a car accident?"

Thomas felt a low simmer begin in his blood. This woman didn't know when to quit. "Look, I don't talk about it, so give it up, alright? And if you're looking for anything physical, I'm not interested." He almost ducked under the table waiting for lightning to strike. He would never hire someone for sex, but that didn't keep his mind from imagining all the dirty things he could do to her.

"You certainly know how to kill the chase." She grinned and walked up to him. She was only inches away, and he could smell her again. Roses. He loved the smell of roses. He had even planted two rose bushes outside his porch that bloomed big and white during the summer.

He didn't move. "You're the only one chasing, and what you're chasing is your own tail. I'm not looking to hook up."

At this, she smiled and then laughed. Just the sound of it made him grit his teeth. That kind of reaction was the last thing he needed with any woman.

"Maybe you should try it. It might relieve some of your stress."

Completely flustered, he hung up his pool stick. He didn't bother looking back; he had to get out of there. He was suffocating. In the parking lot, he took a deep breath and fished for the keys in his pocket.

"You can't get rid of me that easily," he heard the woman say. She was right at his side, keeping an easy stride next to him in her four-inch stilettos.

Thomas whirled on her at the back of his car. "What do you want? Do you think I'm really going to believe you want to screw me? Have you taken a good look at me?"

"I told you, I just want to talk." She leaned against the back of his car when they stopped.

"I think I see why you don't have a boyfriend," he mumbled. There was something in her casual pose that caused his spidey senses to tingle. It was almost too casual. As if every movement was thoughtfully composed. The uncertainty in her eyes was what did him in. He knew in that moment she didn't come on to men very often.

Now the question was: Why him?

Her laughter filled his ears again. If he didn't get out of here, and fast, he was going to do something stupid. Like kiss her.

Taking a deep breath, he took a step forward, so they were thigh to thigh. She looked at him openly, waiting, daring him with those blue eyes to do something. He encased her with his arms, his palm flat on the hood of his car, successfully trapping her. He would figure out what she was up to or die trying.

His gaze riveted to her breasts and he leaned forward to inhale her. "I guess you'll do," he whispered through bared teeth.

She smiled and crossed her arms, looking nonchalant. "Don't you think you should tell me your name first?"

"Who needs names? It's obvious we don't need to be friends to do what you want to do."

"You don't intimidate me. And I don't want to have sex with you."

"Do you think I believe that? Are you planning on robbing me blind if I take you home with me?"

She shook her head.

"And you don't cost anything?"

Alyssa rolled her eyes.

"Yes or no."

"No."

"And you don't have a boyfriend who's going to kill me?"

"Nope."

How could he believe anything she was saying? He didn't even know her.

"Who was the guy you were with last night?"

She gave him a triumphant smile. "So you noticed me last night." It was a statement, not a question.

"Hard not to when you were staring at me like the freak I am.

"Who was he?" he snarled.

"I don't like to talk about it."

"Are we playing games now?"

She looked away. "Let's just say he wants a little more than I do at this point in our lives."

"What *do* you want, Alyssa? I don't think I'm real clear on what we're doing here."

"To get to know you. To talk," she said, leaning her

head to the side and studying his mangled face. "Maybe we can go back to your place."

Thomas frowned. "Is this some sort of joke?"

"No." Her frustrated tone surprised him.

He studied her face, and she looked genuinely irritated he didn't believe her.

"Why me?" he demanded. He was maddened at the idea she might actually be interested in him. "There were twenty other men in there watching you with their tongues hanging out. Why me?"

"Because you *weren't* watching me with your tongue hanging out. And besides, I think you've got a story to tell."

Thomas leaned in, inhaling her fresh scent again. Their lips were so close he could feel the puff of each breath. "You think I've got a story to tell?" he asked, looking deeply into her eyes.

Those blue eyes framed with thick, come-hither lashes turned as dark as a raging ocean as they focused on his lips. She nodded.

He hovered there a moment, unsure if he wanted to kiss her for his own benefit or to punish them both. An angry snarl pulled back his lips when he decided against both and whispered, "Get lost. I'm not interested."

ALYSSA MORGAN CALLED to the bartender for a shot of whiskey as Jeff looked at her in concern. "You can't drink, Alyssa. You've never drank before, and I won't let you start now."

Ignoring him, she slumped over and pressed the heels of her hands to her forehead. "I thought it was him, Jeff. I thought we finally found him. He even *sounded* like Chris. If I could just have some sort of closure!" She swiped at the tears.

Jeff declined the whiskey when the bartender sat it

down in front of her. "Hey," she said, feeling an edge of hysteria bubbling inside of her. "I call the shots around here." Then she grinned miserably. "Ha, get it? The shots?"

Jeff rolled his eyes. "Let's go."

"What if we never find him?"

He looked at her. "Then I think you should close the book and move on. It's been a long time."

Alyssa glared at him. Jeff was once Chris's best friend. Over the years, Alyssa feared Jeff had developed feelings for her. The feel of his hands kneading the tension from her shoulders felt too good to brush off, but it was those small gestures that clued her into his unspoken feelings.

But Alyssa knew she could never truly move on until she knew what happened to Chris. And she knew she could never move on with Jeff. Their grief was all that connected them. Once they both found closure, what would be left?

Alyssa's muddled brain barely registered that Jeff had ushered her out of the pool hall and she now sat in his truck.

"Sleeping with you would be a huge mistake, you know that, right?" She kept her eyes trained on the dash in front of her, waiting for his response.

"So you keep telling me," Jeff mumbled, his voice low with some unknown emotion. "I get it, okay, Alyssa?"

"It would kill Chris."

His pursed lips told her he held back what he really wanted to say.

She narrowed her eyes. "So we can't ever be together." Her eyes drooped as exhaustion hit her full force.

"No, we can't," Jeff sighed and pinched the bridge of his nose.

Alyssa decided to leave it alone. The last thing she needed was her only ally in this search to be angry with her. She valued Jeff's unwavering support in the search for Chris, and they shared many good memories of when Chris. Her life wouldn't be the same without him in it.

The next morning, Alyssa awoke with a throbbing tension headache and immediately downed some aspirin. Jeff came out of the bathroom of the hotel room with only a towel around his waist. A blind woman could see how gorgeous he was, made beautiful by hard labor outdoors with his landscaping business, but Alyssa could only wish it was Chris.

Chris never had huge muscles, but he'd held his own. His eyes and smile shadowed anything else physical. Each time Alyssa thought of him, her heart ached to hear his laughter just one more time.

"I need to talk to you," Jeff said, opening his suitcase and pulling out his clothes.

"Why? What's going on?" she asked. They had only been in this small town in Alabama for two days. Why was he packing his belongings? She studied him as she waited for his answer. He finally stopped packing and looked at her.

"I don't think this is any news, Alyssa. But I'm in love with you."

Keeping quiet for a moment, she weighed her next words carefully. "Jeff, I think we've spent a lot of time together. Are you confusing our friendship with love? I mean…"

He shook his head. His palm ran down his face, wiping his expression away. "I know what I feel, Alyssa. I don't expect you to return it. I just thought you might want to know."

"Thank you, Jeff. I love you, too. But my heart belongs to Chris."

Jeff shook his head again and let out a self-deprecating laugh. "So I guess asking you to marry me and start a new life with me would be out of the question."

A gasp escaped her and she clenched her fists until they ached. She stood and walked over to him, glaring.

"How can you even put me in this position? How can you even suggest we forget about finding your best friend? And what do you think he would say if he ever found out you fell in love with me?" Again, Jeff averted his gaze, shifting his weight uneasily.

"Answer me!" Alyssa's voice trembled and panic overwhelmed her. How could he try to do this to her after the hard work they put into finding Chris?

"I just want us to move on," he tried.

"*You* want to move on. I don't! I want him back with us and for our lives to be the way they used to be!" Anger swelled, and she took another step toward him.

"If he's still alive, and I think it's a long shot after so many years, I want to find him just as much as you do. He was my friend."

"And he *is* my husband!"

"And what are you going to do if you really do find him?" Jeff asked. "Hmm? Are you just going to pick up where you left off? Exactly *where* did you leave off, Alyssa? What if, after five years, he doesn't want you anymore, or has a life of his own? He left you for a reason, you know. He could have another wife and kids by now!"

Pain lanced through her. What a hurtful thing for someone who supposedly loved her to say. It just wasn't a possibility that Chris could have moved on. Not after one silly argument. And especially not after sharing the kind of love he and Alyssa had shared.

Tears gathered in her eyes as she looked at Jeff. "If Chris is still alive, I *know* he still wants me."

"Then why are you wasting your time in this little town?"

"Because that man we saw last night might know something."

She hoped, anyway. Even after her conversation with him, she was fairly certain it wasn't Chris. Other than a slight physical resemblance and a voice that sounded similar, there wasn't much the two men had in common.

And even those things could be wishful thinking after five years of faded memory.

"Either way, it doesn't change the fact that I still love you. I won't stand in your way, but I can't keep coming with you. I have a business that needs me, and I'm not sure I can honor the promise I made to myself not to push you for more."

"There's nothing to push, Jeff. I love Chris, not you."

She knew the words hurt him. His Adam's apple bobbed as he swallowed, then nodded solemnly.

Was she making a mistake? Not once had she entertained a relationship with Jeff; his presence was always one of comfort. But she did wonder if it was time to give up and move on. Not with Jeff, but just gather the pieces of her life and start looking forward.

The magnetic pull she felt toward the man at the bar last night had reminded her she wasn't dead. She was still a woman, despite his rejection. Getting information out of him had become a game of cat and mouse, one she found she enjoyed once she realized he wasn't Chris. Even his brusque behavior was attractive. She barely even noticed the heavy scars lining his face.

While she was lost in thought, Jeff came to stand before her. His large hands cupped her face, and he looked deeply into her eyes. "I love you," he whispered urgently.

Before she could reply, his lips descended on hers, soft yet demanding. For a moment, Alyssa allowed his kiss. She wondered if she would feel a spark of anything toward Jeff. But just as she suspected…nothing.

Pulling away, Alyssa placed her fingertips on her lips. "I can't, Jeff."

He held his hands up as if she aimed a gun at him. "I'm sorry."

"No, I am. I know I've been crazy the last five years searching for him, but if the situations were reversed, I wouldn't want him to stop looking for me. You were his best friend and I guess it's only natural for you to feel something for me. Maybe even an obligation to pick up where he left off. But I don't feel that way about you."

"I *do not* feel an obligation toward you." Jeff angrily stalked across the room and continued to stuff his clothes in his suitcase. He shot Alyssa an accusing look.

"I wish things could be different. With any luck, the man at the pool hall last night will know something. He didn't want to talk about his scars, but I'll wear him down eventually. Maybe then, we'll have answers." Alyssa wasn't quite sure how she was going to pull that off considering he wasn't very social. Nor did he appear to be the kind of man who would take kindly to her marching up to him saying, "Hi, I need to know if you know my husband."

No, this man was a ticking time bomb and if she wanted to get into his good graces and find out if he knew anything, she'd have to play her cards right.

Across the room, Jeff's shoulders slumped in defeat. "I didn't mean for you to think I don't miss him, Alyssa. I just feel like we're spinning our wheels, you know?" His gaze traveled over her face and a soft look came over his features. "Is it so selfish of me to want you for a little while longer?"

She stood, taking her purse, and placed her hand on the doorknob. She narrowed her eyes at him, anger filling her once more.

"Yes, Jeff. Yes, it is."

Chapter Two

THE COOL EVENING breeze offered blessed relief to Thomas after spending the day cooped up inside. He had worked out the majority of his mental frustration at work on some unsolved cases and now he was trying to sweat out his physical frustration in his usual evening jog. Tonight it felt more like a sprint. Even Murphy was having trouble keeping up.

Two weeks had passed since he'd seen the redhead, and yet she still haunted him. He even dreamed about her the previous night, which was probably why he was so set on running right now. In a way, he knew he ran from that vision of her beneath him, her eyes sultry and her lips curving in a sexy grin.

He kicked himself for not taking her up on her offer to come back to his place. Maybe he wouldn't feel so restless if he got her out of his system.

"Come on, boy," Thomas urged the dog with a click of his tongue.

Each foot pounded the pavement in time with his heartbeat. He loved the feel of physical exertion. When he regained consciousness in the hospital after his accident, the doctors and nurses stressed to him that physical activity played a role in his previous life due to the remarkable shape of his body. The nurses researched endlessly and tried to help him trigger memories of a job that required such activity, but his mind remained black. The doctors diagnosed him with retrograde amnesia, with little hope of regaining much, if any, of his memories from before the accident.

In some absurd way, exercise was his only connection to his previous life.

Gritting his teeth he pushed forward, running as fast as he could from those thoughts. He studied the scenery as he and Murphy passed by. His neighbor a few houses down raised his hand in greeting from the seat of his riding mower. Thomas waved in acknowledgment. He closed his eyes at the smell of the freshly cut grass. He loved that smell.

His neighborhood was quiet and he appreciated it on nights like this when he just needed to *be*. He still had the illusion of being a part of the real world, but it gave him the solitude he desired.

Rounding the corner, Thomas almost tripped over his own feet and skidded to a halt. There, about twenty feet off the road, wiggled a familiar behind, clad in denim. The woman attached to it, her hair piled into a great fiery heap on top of her head, was gardening at the house for rent. He glanced over and saw the sign was gone. He hoped she wasn't the new owner!

Mumbling under his breath, Thomas simply stood, unsure of what to do as he watched her. His eyes kept sliding down to those tight jeans. Thomas took a deep breath to calm his libido, reminding himself that this particular woman spelled trouble.

Summoning the anger that kept him sane, Thomas debated what to do. Talk to her? Ignore her? Bake a pie and welcome her to the neighborhood?

Murphy barked when Alyssa sat back on her heels to observe her handiwork. She turned toward the sound and their eyes met. Recognizing him, she smiled. Thomas's lips pressed together. When she smiled like that—much like she had at the pool hall a couple of weeks ago—he rode a fine line between fight and flight. It was like she believed she was the earth and he was the moon. She didn't even look surprised to see him standing there.

Pie baking forgotten, he marched over to her, intent on letting her have a piece of his mind. "Don't tell me you're living here."

Her eyes rounded in perfect innocence, looking at his attire and then to Murphy. "Do you live nearby?"

For a second, his anger faltered. Surely she knew. The coincidence was too much. It didn't matter that he lived in a town with a population of four hundred and his was the only subdivision in a thirty mile radius. "Don't play stupid, it doesn't become you." He propped his hands on his hips, trying to look imposing.

Instead of being intimidated, she took a step forward, licking her lips. "I'm glad we ran into each other again. I think we got off on the wrong foot."

He laughed, although he wasn't amused. "I'll say."

"I had a long day that day," she explained, looking up at him with those pleading blue eyes that brought out an instinct to pull her into his arms. He took a step back.

"Then exhaustion doesn't become you, either."

"I'm sorry. You probably think the worst of me. I'm not normally like that."

"I don't really care how you normally behave. I just want to know why you're suddenly living in my neighborhood."

She looked around, studying her yard and then the house across the street. Finally, her eyes fell on his face. "Do you own the subdivision?"

Thomas stammered. "Well, n...no."

"Hmm," she said, thoughtful again. "I didn't see your name written on this house when I moved in, so I thought it was fair game. Was I wrong?"

He exhaled. "I don't care how you came to live here. I just want to know why."

She raised her eyebrows, her mouth curving into a sexy grin. "Because I needed a place to live."

"Why?" He ground his teeth so hard he feared they would crumble.

"Because I didn't have a place to stay."

His blood pressure was rising; he could feel it in his level of frustration along with his heated face. "You're sassy among other things, huh?"

"What other things?"

Thomas sighed and shook his head. "Let's see, sassy, stubborn, careless, easy..."

Her tinkling laughter filled his ears.

"I might be a lot of things, but I'm not careless or easy."

"You threw yourself at me! If I had brought you home with me that night, you would have slept with a complete stranger."

"Then what does that make you, if you admit you would have gone through with it?"

"Desperate."

Her eyes lowered in shame, giving him a swift kick of guilt in the gut. When she looked at him again, the storm brewing there confused him. As soon as he thought she was going to cry, the look turned sultry, and she grinned. "I know what I want. I don't sleep with just anyone."

"Of course not," he mocked. "Only guys with a mangled face and a bad attitude, right?"

She exhaled. "At least you admit it."

Thomas was tired of the exchange. Verbal sparring intimidated him and his social skills were no match. An image flashed through his mind of tangled arms and legs, something else she might be good at requiring sparring. He clenched his fists tighter. She noticed the movement with her head angled in question but said nothing. Murphy stepped forward and nudged her hand with his nose, and she giggled. She stooped down to pet him and the dog licked her cheek. Lucky mutt.

"How long have you had him?" she asked, twisting her lips to avoid the dog kiss.

"Two years."

"He's a sweet dog."

Thomas grunted in acknowledgment. He shook his head at the strange turn of events in his life. This gorgeous woman confused him. The more he talked to her, the more he didn't find anything suspicious about her, just a woman who was almost as blunt as he was. Did he dare continue talking with her? Was he going to live his life in a constant state of alert?

"Do you want some lemonade?" she asked, giving the dog a final pat on the head, and then standing.

"Do I look like I need some?"

Her eyes traveled the length of him slowly. Her tongue darted out to lick her lips. She snickered. "You look...hot."

He succeeded in stopping the grin that threatened when a new thought entered his mind: What if she just pitied him?

"Well?"

He allowed his eyes to roam her the same way she perused him.

She was shaped like a goddess with that hourglass figure. He could imagine all too well how it would feel to have those legs wrapped around his hips. He cleared his throat. "I need to get back home."

"Got some other easy woman waiting for you?"

"No."

"Then what's the hurry? It's a beautiful evening. Might as well give me some company."

He narrowed his eyes. "I don't think we're looking for the same thing here, lady."

"And what would that be?"

"If you think you're fooling me, you're not. I've seen your kind before. You took one look at me and felt sorry for me. I don't need or want your pity."

"I think you're mistaken. I don't want anything right now but a glass of lemonade." With that she strode away from him and left him to wonder if he'd misread her the whole time.

ALYSSA'S HEART POUNDED out of her chest. This man sounded so much like Chris, it was like stepping back five years. But there were tiny inflections in his voice and phrases that Chris had never used. And anger. The Chris she used to know was always full of breathtaking smiles. This man was full of anger and resentment, and that alone made him seem like a totally different person.

But that voice belonged to Chris.

Even so, she didn't believe he was her husband. And she didn't want to come out and tell him why she lived in his neighborhood. Her need to be with Chris again caused tears to form in her eyes. What if he'd been alone all this time, angry and believing she didn't love him? She didn't often think about the last time they saw each other, but it still affected them, whether he lived or not.

Straightening her back, Alyssa turned to see if he would follow her. He frowned, as if he waged an inner war. In the end, his dog decided for him and bounded after her. When he entered her kitchen, shrinking its size by half with his presence, she poured a bowl of water for Murphy.

"Here you go, big guy," she said as she stooped to place the dish on the floor.

When she rose, the man took a step forward, invading her space. She seized the opportunity to really look at him again. He was around Chris's height and had dark blond hair, but where Chris had thick wavy hair, this man kept it cut short. Chris's gorgeous blue eyes were pale in comparison to this man's black eyes, wrought with suspicion.

She looked at his mouth. If only she could see him smile. Chris's smile was one of the things she would never forget about him.

But here she was confusing the two men again, when she knew there wasn't a connection. The man didn't even recognize her!

As her gaze moved up to his face, he watched her with an unnerving intensity. "Well?" he asked.

She swallowed back the lump in her throat. She wanted Chris back so badly she was trying to morph someone else into him. She reined her tears back since he already thought the worst of her. "Well, what?"

"Are you just going to stare at my imperfections or are you going to offer me some lemonade?"

Alyssa gave him her best smile, trying to cover her insecurities. "Would you like some lemonade?"

He didn't respond, but she caught the way he shuffled his feet in nervousness.

"Are you going to tell me how you got those scars?" she asked, keeping her back to him.

"Are you going to tell me why you're so interested?"

"Why don't we start with your name? Can you at least give me that much?" Alyssa turned and handed him the glass, then she placed her hand on her hip, waiting.

"Will that make us friends if I tell you?"

"Are you going to quit answering all of my questions with a question?" She saw the twinkle in his eye just before he blinked it away.

Alyssa turned and walked out onto her porch. The man's heavy footsteps fell behind her and relief settled in her stomach when he sat on the opposite rocker. Murphy lay down at his feet and closed his eyes.

"Do you always run in the evening?"

"Do you always ask so many questions?" He turned narrowed, annoyed eyes on her.

Alyssa pressed her lips together and gazed out to the road. A group of kids rode their bikes past. Content with only the man's presence, she sipped her lemonade. But it saddened her how he had shut himself off so much. One second he engaged in playful banter and the next was unapproachable.

The man cleared his throat and put the empty glass down with enough force she was surprised it didn't shatter. Alyssa turned wide eyes on him, unsure of his mood. All she could see in those dark eyes was sorrow rooting deeper than probably even he realized.

"My name is Thomas. Welcome to the neighborhood." Standing, he made a long-suffering noise, and Murphy strode down the steps with him.

Panicked at the thought of not seeing him again, Alyssa jumped out of the swing. "Thomas!"

He didn't stop but turned his head.

"Would you like to come over for dinner tomorrow night?"

This halted his retreat, if only for a second. "I'm busy!" he called.

Disappointed but determined, she called back, "It'll be ready by six if you change your mind. I'm making enough for two!"

When he hit the sidewalk, his feet moved into a sprint. With a bark, Murphy took off after him.

Alyssa wasn't sure if she wanted to laugh or cry. Chris would have never turned down a meal with her, even when he was angry. He always said the way to his heart was through her cooking.

But then again, Thomas wasn't Chris.

Alyssa tore her gaze from his lithe body as her cell phone rang. She ran inside to grab it and frowned when the number appeared.

"Hi, Kathy," she said. Chris's mother called her periodically to check on the investigation.

"Jeff called."

"I thought he might."

"Have you found him?" The desperation in Kathy's

voice almost did Alyssa in. Everyone had suffered when Chris went missing, but Kathy suffered the most. No pain compared to that of a mother losing her child.

"I'm checking into a lead, but don't get your hopes up." Alyssa heard a devastated moan. "You always have a lead. And I'm never supposed to get my hopes up. Jeff said he was worried about you being alone, but he had to come home."

Jeff had a big mouth. One that was going to get him in trouble the second this conversation was over. "Jeff shouldn't have called you. I'm fine."

"When will you be home? I don't want you there alone."

"I don't know. But I'm safe..." She trailed off, debating how much to tell her. "Please don't worry."

"How could I not?"

"Because I said so. Once I'm done talking to Thomas, I'll be heading home."

"I don't understand," Kathy finally said.

"I met someone that our private investigator thinks might know something. His name is Thomas. But, I think we're jumping the gun even talking about it. I don't know anything yet."

"Listen to me. Jeff said you're staying there for a while. You must be pretty certain."

"I can promise you the second I figure everything out, you'll be the first to know."

"Okay. I'll be waiting for your call."

When she hung up after her conversation with Kathy, Alyssa immediately dialed Jeff's number. "Where are you?" she demanded when he answered.

"I'm home."

"I don't want you calling Kathy anymore. I just got off the phone with her. She's got her hopes up that we're going to find something."

"Have you spoken with the guy from the pool hall again?"

"Yes. He just left. I rented a house in his neighborhood."

"You did what!" Jeff's voice blared over the line.

"You heard me. The PI sounded confident we might find something here and Thomas's history is a match. I'll never be able to close my eyes at night without trying to find the answers."

"Well, renting a house is a pretty big step."

"I didn't move in with him, Jeff. But I am hoping he'll come to dinner tomorrow night. I invited him. Maybe I'll approach him then."

"Good for you." Jeff's voice dripped with sarcasm. "What's gotten into you? You're acting like a spoiled brat. I don't like the idea of you getting involved with someone we barely know."

Alyssa sighed, plopped down on her couch and fiddled with a loose thread. "I can take care of myself."

"The way you did just before he left?" Jeff's voice rose with frustration. "I don't understand how you could still be so attached to a man who did that to you!"

"Drop it. You promised."

"Yeah, I promised to never mention it again, but do you think I want to stand by and watch you waste another five years chasing after a man who clearly doesn't want you? *I* want you, Alyssa! I've wanted you for years now."

"Is finding closure about you or is it about Chris?"

"Neither. It's about you."

"I don't love you the way you need me to."

"I get that. I do. But I'm sorry if I'm angry that our lives have been hanging by a thread for so long that I forget what it's like to be normal. I just want to see you happy. It's been a long time since you've been happy."

"Jeff..." She didn't know what to say. She understood what he was saying, but there was nothing left for her to do but stay put and ride this thing out. If Thomas didn't know anything about Chris, it might be time to consider leaving well enough alone. If Chris was alive, he might not want to be found. And if he wasn't...

"I love you," Jeff said, "and I don't care if you ever love me back. I just want us *all* to move on and if that involves Chris, great. If not, at least we can stop living our lives based on 'what if's."

Clearing her throat, Alyssa sat up. "Thank you. But in the meantime, stop talking to Chris's mom. If we don't find answers, it's just one more disappointment for her to have to deal with."

She hung up on him then, afraid if she continued talking, her own spark of hope would soon be snuffed out by reality.

Chapter Three

THOMAS CURSED HIMSELF a thousand times during the short walk from his house to Alyssa's. What was he thinking, showing up at her place for dinner? Curiosity, he supposed, was getting the best of him. Curiosity and shame.

He hadn't left her on the best of terms yesterday. In his feeble attempt to get her to quit prying, he'd gone and scared her with his gruffness. Her eyes had said it all and for some inexplicable reason, it killed him a little inside. Angry with himself, he had left, knowing he was likely to do something rash—like beg her to forgive him. The logical side of him whispered he didn't owe her any explanations. A part of him, what he hoped was the part of him he couldn't remember, told him he should apologize.

Glancing down to his fisted hand at the white roses he picked from his front yard a few moments ago, he rolled his eyes. They reminded him of the way her hair smelled. But at least he could have been a little more creative instead of using simple twine to hold the de-thorned bunch together.

Walking up to the porch of her house, he took a deep breath. He really hoped he didn't screw this up. At the very least, he might be able to call her a friend. He'd only managed to find one of those in five years and his boss tended to keep to himself, even though they occasionally played a game of pool.

It wasn't like he was looking for anything with her. She was a beautiful woman, but he lived with his feet firmly planted in reality. She pitied him. She was one of those self-sacrificing types and he refused to fall for it.

Her door hung open, and he saw her through the screen at her kitchen table, white tissue in hand with closed eyes. He stood still, knowing if he moved she'd spot him. Her quiet sniffs met his ears and did funny things to his stomach. Tears on a woman never got to him; he usually considered it manipulation and walked away. But the soft sobs coming from her were born of pure pain, and he longed to know if it was physical or emotional.

He shifted his weight from one foot to another and a board under his shoe creaked. Alyssa's head snapped up and those tearful eyes focused on him. As she stood, she knocked over a glass of water next to her hand. She ignored it.

"If this is a bad time..." he called, feeling like an idiot with his cheesy flowers and inept social skills. What would Robert Downey Jr. do in this situation?

"No! Thomas, come in. I'm so glad you came!" She opened the door for him and smiled through watery eyes. He wanted to do something—maybe give her a hug? No, that might give her the wrong impression. She dabbed at her eyes with the tissue as he stepped in. Sniffing, she issued no apology and went about like he hadn't just heard her crying the most heart-wrenching cries. He admired her for that.

He looked around the kitchen, shifted his weight uncomfortably, and licked his lips. "Here." He shoved the flowers under her nose. To his horror, her eyes filled again. He was about to take them back when her hand slid over his.

Those eyes, searching his with such sadness, made him un- easy. It was like she was waiting for something, and for the life of him, he didn't have a clue what. "Thank you," she whispered. "White roses are my favorite."

He tried to smile, but his face felt more contorted in a grimace than an actual grin. His cheek muscles were a little rusty. "You okay?"

She waved a dismissive hand and straightened. "The roast has about ten more minutes. I had to run to town for some groceries, so I got a late start. Would you like to join me on the deck for some sparkling cider?"

His eyes narrowed in suspicion. "How did you know I don't drink?"

Alyssa shrugged. "The bartender told me. And I don't drink either." She went into the kitchen. After a while, she said, "I don't have a pretty vase for the roses. This stupid glass doesn't do them justice."

Thomas remained silent, watching her trim the stems of the roses and arrange them. When she was done, she took a dishtowel and turned to clean up the water she'd spilled. His hand shot out and grabbed hers.

"I'll get that." Taking the towel from her, he soaked up the water. He wanted to ask her why she she'd been crying and what *her* story was. He hadn't thought until then that she had much of one, but now he wondered. What a pair the two of them made.

By the time he turned around, she held two champagne glasses full of sparkling cider. He followed her to the back deck, where he took the offered glass from her, careful that their hands didn't touch again. Her smooth skin running along his earlier had made his throat go dry.

For a long while, neither of them spoke. Thomas racked his brain for things to say but came up empty. What did women like to talk about? Clothes? Shoes? He knew next to nothing about either. Themselves? Yes, women liked to talk about themselves. Draining the last of his cider, he cleared his throat.

"You wanna talk about why you were so upset?"

Alyssa averted her gaze and gave a shaky laugh.

"You want to tell me how you got that scar?"

Strike one. He looked out over her yard. The grass was getting high and he wondered for a moment if offering to take care of it would give her the wrong impression. Mowing he actually enjoyed. "Got a mower? I can cut your grass after dinner."

"Thanks for the offer, but I've already hired one of the neighborhood boys for the summer."

He nodded. Strike two. It didn't help that all she did was sit on the lounge chair with her legs stretched out. Her delicate, small feet with pretty pink toenails peeked at him from the end of the chair. Her skin was pale, but the beginnings of a summer tan kissed her nose and shoulders. His hand itched to touch what he knew would feel like satin. She wore long shorts, but they still gave him an eye full.

"I hope you like roast."

Alyssa's voice broke his gaze away from her legs. He grunted in approval.

"More cider?" she asked.

"No, I'll wait for dinner."

Thomas couldn't place why things felt so awkward with her. Yes, she hit on him. Yes, he was socially retarded and felt awkward with anyone. But when he looked at her, his hands went clammy, and his heart accelerated. Her looks were part of it, but he couldn't put his finger on the other part.

"How long have you lived here?" he asked, in a desperate attempt to get her talking.

"A little while now."

Gritting his teeth, he forged ahead. "A couple of weeks? A couple of years? That for rent sign wasn't up long."

She smiled as she pulled her foot up and tucked it underneath her. "You ask a lot of questions."

He frowned, knowing his words were coming back to bite him on the rear. "Are we going to dance around every question or try to get to know each other?" There. That was his last attempt to be friendly, if he could call it that. Anything else was going to be on her. It wasn't easy for him to say much to anyone, let alone put himself out there.

"Well," Alyssa said, swinging those sexy legs over the edge of the chair and leaning toward him. "You tell me. I've been trying to get you to open up to me about that scar since the night we first met."

Thomas tamped down his irritation. She was right, but she just didn't understand that he hadn't told *anyone* other than Jerry, his boss, about what happened to him. He thought about it for a moment and came to the conclusion he could give her small details without having to bare his soul.

He swallowed. "I was in a motorcycle accident."

Alyssa's eyes rounded. "A motorcycle?"

He nodded.

"How did it happen?"

He hesitated. "I was speeding *and* drunk and hit a pothole. Wrapping the bike around a tree wasn't enough. My helmet was too big and flew off. I used my skull as brakes."

Alyssa's hand flew to her mouth and tears gathered again. "I thought you didn't drink."

"I haven't since that day. Now you know why." Thomas swore under his breath and stood. "I'm sorry. I didn't mean to upset you."

"No!" She touched his bicep and pulled herself up, getting so close he could read every emotion in her eyes. And the first one he hated the most.

Pity. The whole reason he could never move past this place in life he was trapped in. The perpetual rock and a hard place.

"Recovery must have been so horrible for you. But I'm sure you have plenty of family and friends to help you through," she said.

He snorted and rolled his eyes, stepping away from her touch. "I have all I need." He didn't like thinking about what family he might or might not have.

"Did you have to go through a lot of therapy?"

He didn't bother to hide his irritation. "Can I ask a few questions now?"

She looked up through the thick veil of lashes. "Sure."

"How long have you lived here?" he fired at her.

She looked up at the fading sky and tapped her chin with her index finger, thinking. "Exactly eleven-point-seven-five days."

His annoyance lowered a notch or two. "Exactly, huh? Is that how long you've been in town?"

"No, I was in town a while before that."

"How long?"

"Nope. You only gave me two answers. Fair is fair."

An invisible heat suddenly settled between them when she leaned her hip against the railing of the deck in front of him. He studied her curves, wondering if the reality lived up to his dreams. Standing only a foot from him, he felt her body radiating fire. For the first time, he thought that maybe she really was attracted to him.

His eyes fell to her lips. What would it feel like to kiss a woman? He knew there was no way he was inexperienced in his some thirty years, but he didn't remember any of it. The logistics of kissing seemed easy, but the mental aspect of it was a whole different aspect. Nerves got the best of him around Alyssa. More than likely, if he ever kissed her, it would be a nose-bumping and teeth-scraping disaster. That was just the way things ended up for him.

"Will you tell me why you were so upset earlier?" This time, he wasn't trying to play verbal games with her. He needed to know. Had someone hurt her?

"I thought we were done asking questions." She gazed out over her back yard and crossed her arms, a classic defensive pose. Thomas could read people's body language better than he could their words, which came in handy on the job. Not everyone said what they meant and meant what they said.

Disappointed, he turned so they stood side by side and lowered his elbows to the railing of the deck, looking out over her simple landscaping. A willow tree was situated next to a small creek that ran along the back line of her property. It was a perfect spot for a picnic.

"My husband left me," Alyssa said suddenly, her stare turning distant. "And I'm just trying to find the pieces of my life again."

"Are you divorced?" Thomas asked. He didn't want trouble from any ex's.

Alyssa smiled distantly. "We're not married anymore, no."

"What happened?" He could sense her need to talk about it now that she was opening up. Giving her the opportunity might give him some insight about her.

"We had an argument. Things got pretty heated between us." She stopped and swallowed. "And he left me."

Thomas's eyes narrowed on her face, looking for telltale bruising. "Did he hit you?"

"No. He was going through a rough patch with his job and things just got out of control. He accused me of things I would never do."

"You're making excuses for him?"

She finally looked at him and shook her head. "It wasn't like that, Thomas. We loved each other. More than anything. He hated himself for believing the lies. I saw it all over his face. And I *know* that's why he left me."

Thomas studied her, trying to figure out if she was even more self-sacrificing than he first thought. This tender, romantic, *scary* side of her made him want to run. If she could make excuses for a man leaving her, Thomas supposed he was the fillet mignon to this other guy's sirloin. At least Thomas was loyal until he had a reason not to be. At least...he thought he was.

"Anyway, I haven't talked to him since it happened," she added.

Words left him. What did she want from him if she loved this other guy so much? "Are you just looking for a rebound?"

She turned her body to face him again. "I'm not sure. Peace maybe? To move on, with or without someone. Either way, I just need…a new life."

"And how do I play into all this?" She smiled sadly. "I don't know yet."

At least she was honest. He cleared his throat and looked away when he felt trapped by her stare. Even though he knew he should run, he suddenly felt the need to hold her and give her what she was looking for. But she was better off without him. What kind of life would they live together, if it ever went that far? In and out of doctors' offices, surgeries every two years, reclusive living, scaring their children and all of their friends.

That was why he never considered getting involved with someone. But Alyssa made him think he should jump through hoops to find a way for it to be possible, and he didn't like it at all. "I'm sorry this happened to you, Alyssa." He wasn't good at much of anything and comfort was probably dead last on his list of talents, but when Alyssa's teary gaze settled on his, and she took his hand with a squeeze, he felt like he might have done something right for a change.

Her hand left him before he could return the gesture.

"The roast is probably done. I better go check it." Her voice sounded dejected and sad. Dredging up the past had a way of settling over one's heart like a rain cloud, ready to let loose any moment. He knew, because he felt that way, too. If his accident had never happened, he would be able to let go and give her what she needed. He'd know how to comfort her without uncertainty holding him back. A kiss or two might have her smiling again, and, at the very least, he could have hugged her.

If the accident had never happened, life wouldn't keep getting in the way. He'd have family and friends who could help her, too. There would be a lot of things he could do differently.

As he turned to follow her, a thought ran through his mind, stopping him cold and sending chills down his spine.

If things had been different, he wouldn't have gone down this particular path or ever even met her. And he didn't like how that thought made him feel.

ALYSSA USED A few moments to regroup as she removed the roast from the oven. Chris hadn't had a motorcycle. That solidified her belief there was no way Thomas was Chris. She tried to remember if Chris had access to a motorcycle through one of his friends or family members, but she came up blank.

Her mind kept going back to his voice. His hair color. His eye color. Brown hair and blue eyes were simple enough to explain; a lot of people possessed those traits. But not that voice.

Frustration gnawed at her patience. She wished Thomas was the kind of man who was friendly enough to open up to her, then she could just ask him about his past and figure out if there was any connection. But so far, he offered precious little and made it clear any details were given on his terms.

Behind her, Thomas cleared his throat. She wiped her eyes dry and turned to face him, smoothing her hands against her pants.

"Dinner's ready," she said softly. Looking at him after the news of his accident was like looking at a stranger. Before his revelation, she could see remnants of Chris in his face. Now, she didn't see anything resembling her husband.

"Smells good." He seemed more nervous now. He shifted his weight and rubbed his hands together, looking lost.

"Thanks. You can have a seat, and I'll serve you."

She heard a chuckle but by the time her gaze snapped back to his, all traces of a smile were gone.

"Don't tell me your ex made you spoon feed him, too."

Alyssa's anger shot up fast and hot. "You don't know anything about him!"

Thomas had the good grace to look chagrined. He held his hands up in defense. "I can serve myself."

She narrowed her eyes. This man she invited into her home— whoever he was—insulted her. "Maybe I like to serve my guests." She lifted her chin, daring him to contradict her.

"You can serve other guests. Not me." He brushed past her into the kitchen with his dominating presence. She watched as he sliced the roast and arranged two slabs on each of the plates she had set out. He dished potatoes and carrots next. She realized then that *he* was serving *her*. "Sit down," he ordered and nodded toward the table.

Baffled at the unexpected gesture, she sat down without any argument. He placed the plate in front of her and lowered himself beside her, forking a mouthful of potatoes first. His eyes closed and he mumbled his appreciation.

It saddened Alyssa all over again to think this used to be Chris's favorite meal. When she was cooking it, she was imagining all the ways Chris used to express his gratitude. They would make love long into the evening and hold each other until the moon shone through their window.

None of that was going to happen, at least not with the man sitting next to her.

Maybe Jeff was right, and she was just hanging onto a dream. It was foolish to rent a house based on a feeling. If Chris was alive, she would have found him before now.

But facing the other possibilities caused her heart to ache so badly she felt nauseous.

"Why aren't you eating?" Thomas asked, his eyes on her plate. She swallowed the lump in her throat. "I'm not that hungry." His gaze traveled up to hers and then settled on her lips.

Despite the scars, Thomas was a handsome man behind the pain. His anger went far deeper than just physical pain. He'd been hurt, that much she knew.

Thomas was in amazing shape, and Alyssa allowed herself to gaze at his hard work. His muscles bulged in all the right places, filling out the simple button up he wore. His thighs pushed against the fabric of his jeans, and she knew instinctively those strong hands would be gentle on her body. He smelled like expensive cologne; she couldn't place it, but she knew it from somewhere.

"What are you hungry for?" he asked, leaning ever so slightly toward her, his eyes growing dark with desire.

Licking her lips, she closed her eyes for a moment as all thoughts of Chris left her memory and heat pooled in her cheeks at Thomas's gaze. It hadn't been long since she felt a man's lips against hers, but this feral attraction she felt for Thomas leaned more toward what she felt toward Chris. Either way, it was nice to feel attractive again.

"Ice cream. I'm hungry for ice cream," she said, wishing she could kick herself. Despite the attraction, she knew virtually nothing about him, and he wasn't too keen on revealing details. She couldn't kiss him, not when Chris could still be out there somewhere.

Thomas reared back but kept his emotions tightly controlled. "Oh. I could run into town if you want."

Alyssa shook her head, confused by this man who could be so angry one minute and so normal the next. "Thanks, but I'll get some when I go tomorrow."

After his knowing eyes looked away, they finished their meal in silence. When Thomas was done, he took his plate to the sink and rinsed it off. He slowly turned back to her, drying his hands on a towel. He kept his gaze on her. "I guess I'll let myself out."

He strode out the door, but Alyssa shot up, catching him on the porch with a touch of her hand. "Thomas, wait." She didn't know what possessed her to make him stop.

Thomas turned.

Curiosity got the best of her. Slowly, she raised her hand to his cheek, needing to feel him. He flinched and grabbed her wrist, squeezing hard, but she wasn't afraid. The strained look on his face told her he was scared enough for the both of them. She pushed against his hold, wanting so badly for him to trust her and let her in. After a few moments, his grasp loosened, and her fingertips touched his skin.

He inhaled sharply as his eyes turned into thin slits.

"Does this hurt?" she asked him, amazed by the smoothness of the taut scars that made one side of his face unrecognizable.

"Some of my nerve endings are still pretty raw," he said quietly, his voice low and raspy.

"Is that a yes?"

"No."

She grinned, continuing her exploration. She trailed her fingertips up to his eye, where the lid was mangled and half closed, then traced around to his nose and then down to his lips, feeling the jagged lines that marred his perfection. If he moved a little to the right, she couldn't even tell he was injured. But if he moved to the left... He was so scarred her heart hurt for him.

All the while, he didn't move a muscle, but kept his jaw tight and his eyes on her mouth. She knew he wanted to kiss her. This tight control in a man who seemed to have no control over his emotions fascinated her.

Finally, very softly, she laid her entire palm on his cheek, and he closed his eyes. His arms came around her waist and hauled her roughly against him. She felt his fingertips digging into her flesh at her hips, his barely contained control echoing in the desperation of his touch. She was still touching his face, when his head descended, his russet hair illuminated by the porch light behind him, like an angel.

She waited. She anticipated. She needed. She suddenly didn't care if Chris was still alive. She lifted her chin to meet his lips. Just when she forgot to breathe, his lips moved past her mouth, directly to her ear.

"Thank you for dinner," he whispered. With that, he released her and strode away.

Chapter Four

LETTING OUT A deep breath, Thomas knocked on Alyssa's front door for the second time in as many nights. He knew he was a fool, but he couldn't quit thinking about her. No invitation for dinner tonight gave him a free pass to come knocking, nor had she led him to believe she might like to see him again.

He was a glutton for punishment, no two ways about it.

Alyssa looked surprised to see him when she opened the door. She opened her mouth to say something, but he knew if he didn't say something first, it was a real possibility it might not get said.

"I wanted some ice cream, and I thought of you, and I know this great little ice cream shop on the mountain that I thought you might like, and I was wondering if you might want to ride with me to get some." The rest of the air in his lungs left him in a quick *whoosh* as he waited. He figured that sentence was the longest he'd ever said in his life. Not only would she think he was socially retarded, she might think he hadn't made it past third grade English.

Even in the silence, he could tell from her face she was thinking of a way to let him down.

He held up his hands. "No pressure. I just thought I'd

ask." The corners of her mouth kicked up, and he hesitated.

"I think I'd like that, Thomas."

He raised his eyebrows and leaned his ear toward her, not sure he heard correctly. "You would?"

At that, she threw her head back and laughed. The creamy, slender curve of her neck brought thoughts of other places he would like to see her flesh exposed that way. He tried hard to dampen his need; she was becoming addictive, and he hadn't even kissed her yet.

Maybe he *should* be pitied.

Disgusted, he was determined to keep himself under control. He turned his attention back to Alyssa, who now studied him with the earlier laughter fading from her face.

"Did I do something wrong?" she asked.

He tried to smile at her, but those muscles refused to cooperate again. "Not at all. I was just making a mental note about something I need to do."

She nodded in understanding. "Let me get my purse." Alyssa grabbed her house keys from table next to the door and locked it behind her. "Where's your car?"

"My house. I live just around the corner."

As they approached, Murphy came running up to Alyssa, standing on his hind legs and placing his paws on her chest.

"Hey, big guy," she cooed and scratched his head. "I'll bring you back some ice cream, but don't tell Thomas, okay?"

Murphy seemed to grin at her with his squinted eyes and tongue hanging out of his mouth as he panted. Thomas issued a quiet command, and Murphy got down and went to lie in the grass. Opening the door of his truck for Alyssa, he suddenly felt like they were on a date. Well, technically it wasn't a date, rather an impromptu invitation, but in eyeing his plain clothing he felt a little inadequate.

Alyssa sat quietly. He chanced a glance at her with

her hands folded in her lap, looking straight ahead. Risking his control, he placed his hand on top of hers. "You okay?"

"Mmm hmm," she chirped, giving him a too-wide smile that seemed a little too forced.

He kept his hand on hers and traced lazy circles with his thumb on her soft skin. After a few moments, she not so subtly moved away from him.

"Don't you think we should talk about last night?"

Thomas could feel the disappointment kicking in. No doubt this was the part where she would say, "It's not you, it's me," and give him some stupid excuse to never see him again.

He leaned back, adopting his usual careless pose. "What's to talk about? Nothing happened."

Her eyes met his briefly, and she shifted in her seat, uncomfortable. "I know, but..."

He waited. And he waited some more. "But...what?"

She worried her lip with her fingers and stared at his front door. He looked at it to make sure they weren't being abducted by aliens or anything. "I'm not sure how long I'm staying in town, Thomas," she said. "We both want something more...physical, but is that smart?"

"No."

He figured his honesty took her by surprise when she looked at him. Honestly, he was surprised, too. Telling her it wasn't smart to be seeing him wasn't exactly the way to a woman's heart.

"What do you mean?"

"Have you looked at me lately? Do you think life would be easy with me?" He cranked the engine and put it in reverse, rolling out of his driveway.

"I think you've looked at your scars long enough that they've morphed into something they're not."

He snorted in disgust. "Or maybe you look at the world through rose-colored glasses."

"Why do you say that?"

"The fact you're sitting in this truck with me tells me all I need to know."

She frowned and shook her head. "I'm not following you."

"Never mind." He wouldn't risk hurting her by confiding his suspicion that she introduced herself to him because of pity. She might not have realized it yet, but he had. As long as he kept his eyes open, he couldn't get in trouble.

As they drove, he wondered if it was possible for them to be friends. She was beautiful, and he was...a monster. He glanced over to her, her red hair piled on top of her head and those ivory legs stretched out in front of her.

He blinked as he envisioned himself over her naked body, those legs bent back to accommodate him. He could hear her moans in his ears as if they were making love right there in his truck. Shaking his head, he swerved. She gasped as he fumbled for control, but he quickly righted the vehicle and shot her a look of apology.

"Sorry," he mumbled. What had happened to him? It was like he was suddenly transported to some other place. "So, uh, how long are you planning on staying here?" he asked, trying to get his mind off that image and what it was causing.

"I'm not sure. I might head south."

"Why south?" He turned into the parking lot of the Little Log Cabin Ice Cream Shop and killed the engine.

She shrugged. "I don't know. Just an idea I had."

"Didn't you just rent that house?"

Nodding, she opened her door. "Let's get some ice cream." He soon learned she loved strawberry. He ordered plain vanilla, a comparison that didn't escape him. He led her to a bench overlooking a bluff. He didn't come here often due to the high teenage population—being around teenagers could get ugly—but the few times he came on weeknights, like tonight, he loved sitting in the quiet and enjoying the view.

The sun was beginning its descent and for a little while, his world was perfect. He didn't think about his scars. He didn't think about Alyssa announcing she might be leaving. He didn't think about this unexpected turn his life had taken. Nature always brought him back down to earth to remind him in the end, he'd go just the way he came.

Alone.

"It's beautiful up here," Alyssa said.

He grunted in acknowledgment and draped his arm behind her. The hot day was waning into a humid evening, but there was a cool breeze coming from the trees on the mountaintop. Looking down at her, he watched her licking her ice cream cone, that pink tongue darting in and out, savoring each bite. He'd seen corny stuff like this on TV before, but now he understood why it was so cliché. There was something erotic about the whole thing. He grinned when he saw a dab of ice cream gather at the corner of her mouth. Yet another corny cliché, but he couldn't stop the urge to kiss it away.

Before he could talk himself out of it, he leaned forward and placed his lips against hers, trailing his bottom lip a little to make sure he got it all. He felt her surprise in her stiff body but caught the tremble in her hand when he touched her. Was that good or bad?

It wasn't enough. The simple touch of lips wasn't going to satisfy him. He tensed his muscles to hold himself back.

Alyssa didn't look at him and, in fact, returned to her ice cream after a moment, completely ignoring the fact his face was still inches from hers.

"Sorry," he said, feeling stupid. "I'll get some napkins."

He returned a minute later, using that time to regain control. He sat on the far end of the bench, keeping himself out of reach and finished off his ice cream. His temper simmered at his own idiocy.

The first night he had met her she had practically thrown herself at him. Then she invited him over and cooked him dinner. She even told him she wanted something more physical in the car earlier tonight. Now, there he was, ashamed he'd acted on something so foolish as the idea she might want to kiss him. He was even more ashamed that he still, after her obvious rejection, struggled to keep his libido under control.

Standing abruptly, he said, "I need to get back home. Got some paperwork I should catch up on."

Alyssa followed him without protest. On their way down the mountain and into the valley where they lived, she finally spoke. "What do you do for a living?"

"I'm a P. I.," he mumbled.

"A what?"

"A private investigator. P. I."

He thought he felt the wind from how fast her head turned to look at him. "A private investigator?"

Thomas raised his brows. "Yeah, got something to hide?"

She swallowed. "No."

For a second he didn't believe her, then he dismissed his suspicious nature and rationalized being a private investigator was a little daunting. It involved searching through people's lives and often finding the dirty little secrets no one talked about. He certainly didn't see the public at its best most days.

When he pulled up to her house, he cut the engine and got out of the car. He walked around to her side and opened the door for her, trying to be a gentleman. He would keep his cool with her from now on.

"Do you have family here?" she asked in the cover of darkness as he walked her to the door. The streetlight two doors down shone dimly, but it was enough light to allow him to make out her silhouette. She rummaged through her purse, trying to find her keys.

"Nope, no family."

She stopped and grew quiet. "Where are they?"

Thomas shrugged. "Around somewhere. I haven't talked to them in a long time." That was as honest as he could get without feeling like he was going to fall into the black hole of amnesia again.

"How long?" she demanded, an odd tone in her voice he'd never heard before.

"A long time." He grew tired of Twenty Questions and moved past her. "Good night, Alyssa."

With his hand on the door handle of his truck, he heard her call his name. He stopped but didn't turn around. "Come back for a second."

A deep breath expanded his lungs, and he prayed for patience. Alyssa certainly knew how to try him. "Yeah?" he asked, returning to the base of her porch.

"Will you kiss me again?" she asked so softly he wasn't sure he heard right.

"You're kidding me." He stepped onto the bottom step and waited.

"No." She didn't sound like she was kidding, but with her, he couldn't be sure.

"You're not the easiest person to read, you know that? You told me on the night we met that you wanted to get to know me, then you cook dinner, accept an invitation to get ice cream, *tell me* that you'd like something more physical, and then you freeze me out when I get near you. What is it, Alyssa? Either way, I can handle it, but I'm beginning to think *you* can't." He stepped up one more step, his anger resurfacing and building.

"I'm sorry. You just caught me off guard tonight. I haven't been close to anyone in a while."

"Either you want me or you don't."

"I know, I just..."

"You just what?"

"I want you to kiss me." Her voice sounded so feeble that the sassy attitude he witnessed when they met all but disappeared. Yet, she still asked. He knew it must have cost her pride a great deal. His anger deflated.

"You want me to kiss you."

"Yes."

"Are you going to kiss me back?"

She hesitated. Then he heard a quiet, "Yes."

"Are you going to invite me in?"

"No."

He almost grinned, but his blood pressure was too high to allow it. At least her honesty hadn't disappeared. It was one of her best qualities.

"So, you just want a kiss." He went up two more stairs and stood so he was eye level with her. The light caught her eyes a little and fear stared back at him. Was she afraid of him? Afraid of whatever she might find in his kiss? He had warned her it wouldn't be easy with him.

"I'm not a nice person, Alyssa. Got lots of baggage. You should probably think twice about this."

"I have. I'll regret it later, but I want you to kiss me. I don't want to think about anyone but you right now."

Was that it? Did she think of someone else when he was around? The ex, maybe?

He closed the distance between them and pulled her into his arms. He took a moment to savor the feel of her soft body against his. "You feel good right here," he whispered, unable to keep his thoughts to himself.

She didn't answer. The short puffs of her breath tickled his neck as he inhaled her rose-scented hair. His eyes drifted closed. Touching his forehead to hers, he grinned. His muscles were finally cooperating with him. Her sweet breath fanned his cheek, and he realized she was waiting. The streetlight caught her eyes again and his breath left him. Desire looked back at him, not fear. He wasn't sure how he knew what desire looked like—TV could only show much. He hoped against hope kissing was like riding a bicycle and even with a brain injury, he hadn't forgotten how.

Tentatively, he lowered his lips to hers. He was waiting for any sign his touch wasn't welcome. A shove, a frozen body, anything. But she still felt warm and limber in his arms, and he allowed his lips to finally caress hers. Her soft sigh fueled his need, and his hold strengthened on her. He angled his head, lost in sensation. The velvet heat of her mouth opened for his tongue, an invitation he took full advantage of. As he swept inside, another flash of her underneath him hit him in the gut as he did so. But it was forgotten when she rose on her tiptoes and molded their bodies together, moaning against his mouth.

There wasn't much left of his control already but when her leg came up and hooked around his hip, he could almost hear it snap. Fumbling toward the wall, which he knew was there somewhere, he intended to pin her against it. His desire turned savage.

He envisioned sweet kisses and touching and whispered sweet nothings with Alyssa. Not this. This feral heat surprised him. They could have burned up, quite literally, and they wouldn't have noticed.

Alyssa kissed him back with equal fervor, and by the time he pinned her against the front of her house, both of her legs had wrapped around his waist. He strained against her, wishing she wore a skirt instead of those shorts.

Breaking free from her mouth, his lips settled over the pulsing vein in her neck, sucking hard as he worked the buttons of her pants.

"Thomas," she gasped, gently moving his hands away.

"I'm thinking we should have done this from day one," he said against her mouth. The back of his mind registered her rejection, but he was too distracted with her body. His hands found bare skin under her shirt and his fingers moved over her back, playing with her bra strap.

"Invite me in," he demanded.

She didn't acknowledge him but continued kissing his neck and scratching her fingernails down his back.

"Invite me in, Alyssa," he said gruffly, feeling a little desperate.

That seemed to cool her down as she pulled away and took a deep breath. "I don't think we should do that."

Talk about a bucket of ice water. "Have you lost your mind?"

Her husky chuckle was cut off by a quick kiss. "I think I just did. But we barely know each other, Thomas."

"True, but remember this was your idea."

"Because I asked you to kiss me?"

"Yes."

She shook her head. "In case you missed it, I liked that."

"I know we're in the dark, and it's hard to see, so we can keep the light off if you'd prefer—"

"Don't ever insult me *or you* like that again. Stopping has nothing to do with your face and everything to do with the fact I'm just not emotionally ready for this yet."

It occurred to him despite his earlier assumptions, maybe she wasn't a one-night-stand kind of gal. "So why were you ready to come home with me that night?"

"I told you, I just wanted to talk. But even tired, I wasn't stupid." She kissed him lightly. "I knew from the second I looked at you it would be like this between us."

Thomas lowered her legs, making sure she slid down every inch of him. With a sigh, she gave him a languid kiss, as though this was something they'd done together for years. It was a nice thought, but not one he lingered on for long.

"So..." he whispered, pinning her against the wall with the lower half of his body. "Why don't you give me a call when you decide you're ready? In the meantime, I've got a cold shower waiting for me at home."

Thomas pushed away from Alyssa after a final kiss, her soft laughter filling his ears all the way to his truck.

Chapter Five

"JEFF, WHY ARE you calling me again?"

"I wanted to check in on your progress," Jeff said, sounding hurt. Alyssa hated that speaking to Jeff was so hard after meeting Thomas. Everything felt misplaced between them now when all she could think about was Thomas's kisses.

"Didn't I tell you I would call if I had any news?"

"Yes, but—"

"Stop calling me, Jeff."

His long-suffering sigh met her ears. "Alyssa, do you realize I want to find him, too?"

"You certainly didn't give me that impression when you were packing up your stuff to leave."

"I know. I'm sorry. I just have to make sure my business stays on its feet, or we won't be able to fund these trips anymore."

The wind blew out of Alyssa's sails. She didn't know what to think anymore. "Thomas isn't Chris. He told me he was in a motorcycle accident. Chris didn't have a motorcycle and as far as I know, none of his friends did, either."

There was a long silence. "Do you know for sure it was a motorcycle?"

"That's what he told me. He doesn't have any reason

to lie." Alyssa examined her nails and thought again about Thomas's touch. Her cheeks flushed as she exhaled.

There was an unrecognizable tone in Jeff's voice when he spoke next. "Where are you going now?"

That was a very good question. She didn't really know. The thought of leaving Thomas did funny things to her stomach. She couldn't keep up the charade much longer, though. Eventually she'd have to choose. Chris could still be out there waiting for her, alone, and she had to find him. Until she had solid proof Chris was dead, which was a shot in the dark after so many years, she would never give up. Someone somewhere knew something. But being with Thomas made her feel alive. She could feel her heart beating again and her senses seemed heightened. What if this was a sign she should begin the process of moving on without Chris?

"I don't know, Jeff. I'm not sure I'm ready to leave here, yet."

"Have you slept with him?"

Alyssa stood up from the couch where she sat. "That's none of your business." Her flat tone did nothing to convey her fury and intentionally so.

"Just make sure you're careful. A man like that could be volatile."

"Thanks for the warning. I need to go."

"I don't want anything to happen to you." His low, defeated voice played on her sympathy, but she realized it was exactly what he wanted. Jeff normally didn't act so spoiled, but she went too far and encouraged something that shouldn't have been started in the first place. She loved Jeff for being such a wonderful friend for Chris, but there was nothing beyond that.

"Goodnight."

When she hung up, she felt the urge to see Thomas. Throwing on her shoes, she took off at a sprint. Maybe being with him would help her find some of the answers she sought.

Knocking on his front door, she heard Murphy scurry to the other side and bark. She waited, but Thomas never answered. After knocking three times, she gave up and returned to her car.

Was he at the bar? In her desperation, she drove to the place they first met. A quick glance around told her he wasn't there either. Was he okay? She knew he worked, but the unexplained fear in her heart scared her. Had he noticed her hesitation when she found out he was a private investigator? Was he out investigating her background right now?

Alyssa couldn't dwell on the fact that, despite not knowing much about Thomas, he could already be involved with someone. That was something she cleared up for him on her personal life, but he hadn't talked much about his own.

Letting out a frustrated sigh, she left the bar, knowing she shouldn't be this interested in him. The man screamed *issues*. But at the oddest times, she felt this undeniable connection with him, not only physically but mentally. It was as if he understood her.

She drove by Thomas's dark house one more time before pulling into her driveway, exhausted. But she didn't go in when she arrived. Instead, she sat on her porch swing in the dark, wondering how her life suddenly became so complicated.

She thought of Chris, of his beautiful smile and handsome face. She thought of how happy they used to be. Six months before he disappeared, they rescued a puppy together and named him Dax. Two years ago, Dax moved in with Chris's mother when Alyssa took her search to a higher level.

As her smile faded, she remembered the night Chris left and their terrible fight.

FOR OVER A year, Chris's landscaping business had struggled, and he was at the breaking point. All of their money was spent trying to stay afloat and their house was on the verge of foreclosure. Their only car broke down every time Alyssa drove it further than to work and back.

"I'm closing the business, Alyssa," Chris had said that evening. "What? No! You can't, Chris. This is your dream." Alyssa remembered all too well the panic she felt at his news.

"I have to. There's no way we're going to make it otherwise. I have to get a real job."

"Chris." She placed her hand on his arm. He shocked her by jerking away from her touch and moving out of reach. The pain of the rejection hurt her more than anything.

"This is just too much right now. Jeff and I had an argument. I have to do what's best for us, and it's not chasing a dream right now. I've left you alone for too long, and it's all my fault we're in this mess."

"What's best for me is for you to be happy. And you won't be happy doing anything else."

Alyssa's jaw dropped at the anger on his face when he turned. "No, I won't be happy doing anything else. But I've got more to think about than just myself, Alyssa! Have you taken a good look at our life lately? You're gone all the time! We never see each other. I want to be someone you can love again." He hesitated but didn't go on. Alyssa got the sense he wasn't saying something.

Chris hadn't, until this point, said he wasn't happy with her, nor did she ever think about being with someone else. "I've never once led you to believe that I wasn't happy. And I do love you, Chris. More than anything. Where is all this coming from?"

"Every time I turn around you're leaving. We never make love anymore, spend time together, nothing. It makes me wonder if someone else is making you happier." He watched her carefully.

"You think I'm cheating on you? I have friends who invite me out, or I go to their house to talk. Do you think because we're married I should stop talking to them? I hate my job, I hate never seeing you anymore, but our life together means more to me than anything else. I would never do what you're suggesting."

Tears slid down her cheeks, and she turned away from him, but he wasn't done. With red cheeks and flashing eyes, he took a step forward. "Don't try to manipulate me with your tears. I followed you, Alyssa. I saw you with Jeff at your friend Natalie's house. I saw the way you looked at him. It was the way you used to look at me. Don't lie to me anymore."

"I'm *not* lying to you." Alyssa thought back desperately to what he could have seen. Then she remembered a few weeks ago she went to Natalie's when Jeff had been there.

"I saw the way you greeted each other. You jumped into his arms. He put his arm around you and kissed your forehead. And then you reached up and held his hand as you walked upstairs to Natalie's apartment. I might be stupid, but I'm not blind."

"What do you want me to say, Chris?" she held out her arms, waiting for him to answer. "You're wrong." Yes, they had embraced but they always gave each other a hug when they saw each other.

"Jeff admitted he was in love with you, Alyssa." Tears formed in his eyes, and he pressed his lips together.

"I don't know how you could believe something like this about me. I would never—"

"Because I don't know who you are anymore! I don't know who I am! I've lost my job, my wife, and the only life I ever wanted to someone I thought was my best friend! I hope Jeff loves you the way I should have."

Chris threaded his fingers through his hair in a frustrated motion and turned his back to her. He walked over to their china display and picked up a plate, turning it over. Before Alyssa knew what he intended, Chris hurled the plate at the wall across from them. She watched it crumble into tiny pieces.

"That was a wedding present!" A sob tore from her throat. Her heart ached for Chris, who was clearly hurting, but she was clueless on how to prove to him that she hadn't cheated with Jeff. He studied her for a moment before the anger claimed his features again. His mouth cinched as he pointed an accusing finger.

"Some commitment our wedding day turned out to be. Till death do us part, huh?" He shook his head and snarled, "I can't do this right now. I need some air."

"You think that leaving me is going to change anything? Jeff will tell you that we're not sleeping together." This time, it was Alyssa who pointed the finger and poked him in the chest, her voice a crescendo as she continued. "You stood in front of God and said you'd honor me, and *this* is not honor! You're the biggest liar I've ever laid eyes on!"

"Takes one to know one, baby."

Chris's hands shook, and they fisted and released at his side. Alyssa glanced quickly at them. The tears dried and a solemn acceptance took their place. He needed some time to sort through things and get his head on straight.

She made sure her eyes were holding his. "On second thought, I think it's time you leave. Some air will do you good."

Chris's throat worked as he swallowed. The anger was gone. He looked as though he was on the verge of tears as he took a step forward.

"Just leave," she insisted. "We'll talk about this when you've thought about it rationally." She needed some time to calm down, too.

JUST NOT FIVE years.

Was she a fool to still be searching for him? When she thought back to that night, she could hear the immaturity of their conversation, the uncertainty of their future. Their six years of marriage had been great until that point, maybe even a little too good. They fought occasionally, but nothing like that night. And not once had they questioned fidelity. Even after all this time, she still felt nauseous when she thought about it.

Maybe after he left her, he moved to some exotic island and found another wife. Or perhaps something bad really happened to him. But the truth was, she just didn't know. Every private investigator came up empty.

She thought for a moment about hiring Thomas. But what could a small-town PI find that the reputable New York investigator couldn't? She pushed the idea aside, rose from her swing and went inside.

Alyssa didn't know many things, but she knew she wanted to see Thomas. She had to make sure he understood why they couldn't continue down the path they were on.

She wasn't free to be with anyone else until she found the answers she needed.

THOMAS SIGHED AND rolled the stiffness out of his neck. Cheating wives were the worst. Sitting outside the hotel for the last four hours was putting him in a bad mood. It was past two in the morning and when these people cheated, they went all out. He could just imagine the amount of Viagra it took to justify spending the money these men spent on hotel rooms.

His mind wandered to Alyssa for the thousandth time. There hadn't been much time for him to call her and tell her he would be gone tonight. After they parted ways the previous night, he was afraid his lack of contact would make her think he wasn't interested.

Was he? Did he really want the complications this woman brought? And there was that guy at the bar. He wasn't sure if he was the ex or not. He needed to ask. She probably had baggage from the marriage, which he was sure was more than she claimed.

Physically, it was safe to say he was attracted. Their little scene last night on her porch was quite the testament to that. And he didn't have any doubt that she was attracted to him now. Women might be good at faking some things, but Alyssa hadn't been faking the look in her eyes as she locked him between her legs last night. He would have been a happy man if she had invited him in, but instead he wound up laying in his bed after a cold shower thinking about all the possibilities.

He didn't like thinking like that, either. His warning apparently wasn't enough to keep her away. Didn't she realize that everything about him was abnormal, from his ugly face down to his social inabilities? But he resolved to think long term, for her sake. Little by little, they'd be forced into an even greater life of seclusion because of her shame of him.

Keeping his eye trained on the cheating woman's car, he grabbed his cell phone and dialed his boss. It might be late, but he knew he'd still be up.

"Get him yet?" Jerry asked without an introduction.

"No."

"Then what's up?"

"I'm thinking too much."

"Got anything to do with that redhead?" Thomas thought he could detect a smirk in Jerry's voice, but he couldn't be sure.

"How did you know?" "It's a small town."

"It was that bartender at the pool hall, wasn't it?"

This time Jerry chuckled. "Yeah."

"What did he tell you?"

"Not much, just that he hadn't seen you in a few

nights. Then he saw her in there tonight looking for someone, and he assumed it was for you."

Thomas let out a breath. "I knew I should have called her."

"What do you know about her?"

"Not a whole lot. She just moved here and has an ex-husband. I don't think she's told me the whole story."

"Are you going to ask her out?"

Thomas sighed. "I think we're a little bit past that."

"You've slept with her already?" Jerry sounded impressed.

Thomas laughed. "Not quite. And that's why I'm hesitating... and thinking too much."

"I don't see why you should hesitate over that."

"There are a lot of good reasons."

"Well, I'll tell you what I told my nephew a few months ago about his girl trouble. One day at a time, man."

Thomas mulled this over while continuing to eye the car. "I think I took it a *year* at a time. I'm having feelings about her I've got no business having this early in the game. Talk about head trauma."

Jerry chuckled. "You'll figure it out."

Thomas sat up. "Gotta go, the woman's coming out of the hotel." He exited the call and grabbed his camera, but his mind never strayed from a cute redhead that made his stomach feel like he was on a roller coaster.

A KNOCK DOWNSTAIRS woke Thomas the next morning. After getting home only a few hours prior, he was not happy that someone, more than likely a Jehovah's Witness or a girl scout, was banging on his door. He threw on a shirt and shorts just as the noise started up again.

They were persistent; he'd give them that.

Unlocking the door after tripping over Murphy, he

swung it open, ready to give the annoyance a piece of his mind. But standing there, looking fresh as a dewdrop with damp, fiery hair flowing around her face was Alyssa. She wore no makeup and that form-fitting shirt didn't do much to keep his mind from thinking about how it felt to have her against him.

"Hey," he grunted as he shielded his eyes from the bright morning sun.

"Hi."

His brain wasn't working yet, but he noted her nervous body language in the way her eyes darted from his skewed hair, to Murphy's sleeping body, to the living room behind him. Did she think he had someone with him?

He frowned but then after a moment, it kicked in. Jerry mentioned she was in the pool hall looking for him last night, and he hadn't called her. Now he was sleeping in late. "I meant to call you, Alyssa." He bit his tongue. That sounded like an excuse if he ever heard one. "I was working late," he tried again, but she held her hand up to stop him.

"I don't need any explanations, Thomas. We need to talk." His eyebrows rose. "You sure do like to talk."

"I'm serious," she said.

"So am I."

What was he supposed to do? He didn't remember ever being in a relationship before, if that was what you could call this. After their near physical combustion, did that put them on a new level? Was he supposed to pull her in his arms and kiss her? He took a step closer, and she shot him a warning glare.

He'd take that as a no. "What?" he asked.

"Could you come over to my house for lunch?"

"Are you trying to fatten me up?"

"Can you please be serious here?"

"Why don't we go out somewhere? It's Saturday, we could catch a movie after lunch."

She was shaking her head before he was done. "I can't."

"Wanna tell me why? Isn't that what I'm supposed to do? Ask you out on dates for dinner and a movie?" He leaned against the doorframe, crossing his arms over his chest and his bare feet at the ankles.

"No."

Now what? Did he try to get her to talk or leave it alone? He could already tell he wasn't going to be any good at chasing; he didn't have the patience for it. "Jerry told me the bartender saw you in the pool hall last night looking for me."

"Who's Jerry?"

The wind blew and the smell of roses drifted to him. He wasn't sure if it was from his bushes a few feet away or the shampoo Alyssa used. Either way, he closed his eyes, momentarily enjoying the smell.

"My boss," he said when he opened his eyes. "You smell really good." His voice went deep as he murmured the words and took her hand in his.

"Thomas..."

He saw her resolve weakening in her slumped shoulders, and he tugged on her arm, making her stumble to him. He reached up with his free hand and tugged at a strand of hair. "I love your hair."

"We really need to talk," she insisted, her voice holding an edge of panic.

"Are you afraid of me?" The thought alone scared him, but with his scars, it was always a possibility.

"No."

"Do you really think I was out with another woman last night with this face? I hate to break it to you, but the ladies aren't exactly knocking down my door."

"No, I believe you."

"Then why are you acting so weird around me all of a sudden?" She shrugged, her blue eyes finally meeting his, stealing his breath. She bit her bottom lip and he felt a tug of tenderness in his chest.

He couldn't think of anything to say to her other than, "Kiss me."

Alyssa hesitated again, and he remembered his own hesitation two nights prior. It was a big hurdle to leap over, but he thought she might feel better if she felt like she controlled some of the action.

"Thomas, I don't think that's a good idea."

"It's not. But kiss me anyway," he whispered, his tone soft.

She licked her lips, and he waited. She leaned forward and he cupped her cheek gently, letting his breath out slowly when their lips met. He allowed her the freedom to explore, and she did so, meekly at first. When she realized he wasn't going to inhale her, her lips pressed harder, and he opened for her. Her sweet tongue darted in his mouth and retreated before he could catch it. When it didn't return, he followed her and swept inside of her mouth. Her sharp intake of breath and her fisted hand clenching his shirt told him she liked that, so he did it again. And again. Before he knew it, she wrapped her arms around him and pushed her body close.

Trying to keep his wits about him, he held her, his hand exploring her back. The goal here was for her to feel comfortable with him, not to feel preyed upon. If he moved from his casual pose against the door to press against her, he'd be lost. He could have her in his bed within a few seconds before she so much as batted an eyelash.

It was the thoughts of his bedroom just up the stairs that made him wind down the kiss. The last thing he wanted to do was screw this up, physically or emotionally.

She made a tiny protest in the back of her throat when he pulled away. Trailing the back of his finger down her jaw, he grinned at her.

Looking up at him through a sexy haze, she smiled back. "You're so handsome when you smile at me like that."

His smile fell. He dropped his hand to his side. "I might be a lot of things, Alyssa, but handsome isn't one of them." He pushed away from the door, but her hand on his arm stopped him.

"Scars are just scars, Thomas. They don't change who you are on the inside."

He shook his head. "What if I don't know who I am?"

Rounded blue eyes met his in surprise. "What?"

"Nothing. I'm just saying that the scars have certainly changed my ability to see things through rose-colored glasses the way you do."

"Why do you keep saying that? I don't look at the world through rose-colored glasses any more than you do."

"C'mon, Alyssa. Handsome? You have to be blind to call someone like me handsome."

"What if it's not just about your face? I might not know what I want from you, but I do know I like everything about you. What little you've let me see is amazing."

His heart thudded in his ears. She really was clueless about him. "What if there's a side of me you don't know about? What if that side of me isn't so wonderful?"

She smiled patiently. "It doesn't matter."

He nodded. "It does matter, trust me." Full of hatred for the accident and all it left him without, he wrenched away from her and went out on the porch, sitting on his swing. "But you're leaving, right? What's the use in all this anyway?"

She sat next to him and her palm rested on his thigh in a reassuring way. "Thomas, there are things about me that you don't know, either. Don't think you're the only one with problems."

He didn't say anything to keep from losing his temper.

"Will you just come to my house for lunch? Maybe we can figure out what's next."

His eyes bore into her shimmering, blue ones. "I don't think figuring things out is what I need right now."

He eyed her pointedly, shifting his weight in the swing to accommodate the effects of her kiss.

Abruptly, she stood and walked away. "Fine. Have it your way."

If Alyssa expected him to follow her and beg, she was sorely mistaken.

Chapter Six

ALYSSA COULDN'T HELP the anger boiling inside her. It seemed to be the only emotion that made sense. Thomas was a stubborn fool if he thought he was going to sleep with her so soon. He was nothing but a deterrent in her search for Chris, one that possessed the ability to make her forget Chris completely. Somewhere along the way, her focus had shifted from finding Chris to thinking about Thomas constantly.

She vigorously scrubbed her counter tops in her kitchen, trying to wipe away the confusion she felt. Her life was upside down. Even worse, she wanted to go back to Thomas's house and make sure he understood she wasn't looking at the world with rose-colored glasses. How could she with the kind of life she lived?

Aside from anger and confusion, Alyssa felt lost. Before Jeff left and she rented the house in Thomas's neighborhood, she had had purpose. Now, she lingered for Thomas with no real motivation aside from the promises of his kisses and his companionship. She shrugged, pressing her lips together. So she'd stay. That didn't mean that she couldn't keep looking for Chris. And she would slow things down with Thomas, too.

Alyssa sighed. She was a mess. All she really wanted, when she was honest with herself, was for Thomas to

come over and hold her and help her through this crazi-
ness she found herself drowning in. They didn't have to
be involved or feel strained to take things any further.
They could just be friends.

Couldn't they?

When Alyssa remembered those blue eyes boring into hers with delicious promises, she knew she was fooling
herself if she thought Thomas wouldn't press the subject.
He was a virile man and despite his claims otherwise,
handsome. Even the scars didn't keep her from seeing
what an amazing person he was.

Shaking her head, she told herself it didn't matter.
Honorable or not, he kept her from finding Chris. When
she was with Thomas, she all but forgot about him, which
brought her to her next overwhelming emotion.

Fear.

What if Jeff was right and she really should give up?
She tried to keep the possibility Chris might have left her
for good at the forefront of her mind. The nagging feeling
in her heart told her he was still alive, out there somewhere, but the idea he didn't want to be found hurt her.
How would she cope with that if it was true?

Alyssa went back to her initial thought that Thomas
could be Chris, but quickly dismissed it. He kissed
differently, held her differently. While his build was
similar, Thomas was bigger and stronger. Very little about
the man triggered much hope he had any information
now that she knew him better.

She couldn't stop thinking about the first night she
saw him in the bar, keeping his scarred face away from
the crowd. The profile from his good side *was* Chris, if
only for a moment. Had her imagination run wild? It was
all she could do not to run to him, screaming at the top of
her lungs she'd finally found her husband.

Then he turned. She saw the ugliness and the pain;
the accusing eyes that looked at no one, kept to himself,
ashamed and embarrassed, blaming the world for his

pain. In that moment, Alyssa shed a tear for a man she didn't know, for crushed hopes that her search might come to a close.

It was that first reaction when she had seen his good side that kept her involved with him, riding on the chance he might somehow be connected to her ex-husband, even in some small way. Hope burned eternal and all that, even though her mind claimed otherwise.

"You win, I'm here. Now what are you going to do with me?" A deep voice behind her said.

Alyssa jumped and spun around. Her hand flew to her chest. Thomas stood behind her with crossed arms and narrowed eyes. She couldn't speak since the air left her lungs. So engrossed in her own thoughts, she hadn't heard him come in.

"Well?" he pressed with raised brows.

Alyssa dragged in a deep breath. "You just scared ten years off my life!"

He pointed his thumb over his shoulder. "Yeah, you should probably think about locking your door occasionally. Anybody could just come walking in."

Alyssa rolled her eyes but her determination was renewed. This couldn't go on anymore. She and Thomas were a disaster waiting to happen. "What are you doing here?"

He looked around the kitchen and then at her table. "You invited me to lunch. I'm here to eat. I'm hungry."

"The invitation doesn't stand anymore."

"Too bad, I walked all the way down here for lunch, and I'm staying until I get it." Thomas pulled out a chair, turned it backwards and took a seat, watching her with expectant eyes.

"You practically live in my back yard. It was no hardship to walk here."

"Well," he sighed as he crossed his arms and propped his chin on muscle. "That's my story, and I'm sticking to it."

Alyssa could be more stubborn than him. She folded her arms and mimicked his pose, one eyebrow rising in his direction.

"Better get a move on, time's ticking." He pointed to an imaginary watch on his wrist.

Without another word, Alyssa walked past him into her living room and sat down in the recliner, pushed out the foot rest, and gave him a pointed look. She grabbed the book she had been reading the night before and tried to concentrate. Thomas tapped his foot in a distracting staccato, but she refused to budge.

After a few moments, she heard him ask, "How many times have you read the same sentence?"

She was *not* going to smile at him. She bit the insides of her cheeks. This was Thomas's way of testing her. She knew that because of the way he'd reacted at the thought of her serving him their first dinner together. "How many times do you think you'll have to take a cold shower?" she retorted.

"Oh, honey," he drawled. She heard his footsteps as she continued staring at the page in front of her. He stood in her peripheral vision for only a moment. His leg swung over, and he straddled the footrest of the rocker. He leaned down and pushed the chair into the reclining position as far as it would go. They were practically nose-to-nose when he gently lifted the book from her hands and put it on the table next to her. "I'm a patient man."

She frowned up at him. "Funny," she replied. "You and patience seem to go together like oil and vinegar."

The grin he gave her was predatory. "Would you like for me to show you what really goes together?"

Alyssa pointed over his shoulder. "The shower is up-stairs."

"Wanna join me?"

She gave him a sweet grin. "Cold is to the right."

The twinkle in his eye indicated he was enjoying their exchange. Truth be told, Alyssa found him incredibly sexy when he spoke to her that way, all low and raspy and suggestive.

Once again, Alyssa realized Thomas was distracting her from finding Chris. She should be doing research or something, looking for a new lead or calling the private investigator in New York that had taken her money and disappeared.

Pushing past him, she walked into the kitchen and gathered the items they would need for lunch. She slapped them down angrily on the counter tops, wishing her emotions would settle on something constant.

"Here's the bread, and everything else you need. Fix your own sandwich." She turned to get away, but instead ran straight into the hard wall of his chest. His arms locked around her, and she pushed at him, her attempt feeble in lieu of his strength.

His eyes smiled down at her, focused on her mouth.

She felt like she was being torn in two, half of her devoted to finding Chris, the other half going for the worm, being lured by the thrill of all Thomas represented. A new life. A new beginning.

"Would you have a picnic with me out by your creek?"

Alyssa's gaze looked out over her yard to the perfect spot. She wanted to say no, just to keep her sanity. Her original plan to tell him whatever they were doing couldn't continue went up in smoke right before her eyes. "Sure."

"I'll fix the food. You get a blanket." Thomas kissed her nose and swatted her behind as she pulled out of his arms. She shot him a look of warning, but he just grinned at her charmingly, unaffected by her threat.

Giving in just this once, she grinned back at him and went upstairs to find a blanket.

"So what do you do for a living?" Thomas asked when they were outside as he leaned back on his elbow and chewed on an apple.

Alyssa followed his movements and watched as his strong jaw chewed. His eyes sparkled in the afternoon sun and his brown- blond hair glimmered. Those full lips worked and moved as he ate, and she felt a blush creeping up her cheeks when she realized she was imagining those lips against her skin.

"I...um." She cleared her throat. "I have a degree in education. I'm going to find a teaching position as soon as I'm settled somewhere."

Thomas studied his apple intently. "So what's it going to be, Alyssa? Are you staying or are you going? Surely you know by now."

Alyssa watched the trickling water flowing over a smooth pebble and thought about how it compared to her life. The once rocky, jagged stone had been smoothed away by the water with time, washing away the sharpness. Had time slowly washed away her pain? Was Thomas the man she was meant to move on with? The ache in her heart grew when she thought about leaving him. Even though they didn't know each other that well, she was unable to see past the day and how it didn't seem complete without Thomas in it. She wasn't sure how she felt about any of it yet, but that was the story of her life. One day at a time.

With a deep breath, she lay down on the blanket and waited until he looked at her. He swallowed and focused his gaze directly on her. "I think I want to stay."

"Are you sure about that?" He grinned when she nodded. His hand reached down and threaded and unthreaded their fingers. The thrill she felt every time they touched jolted her senses. She closed her eyes, his strong hand trailing up her arm and settling on her cheek. Her eyes fluttered opened and settled on his mouth. "I'm glad you're staying," he whispered. Tenderly, he leaned forward and pressed his lips against hers.

His kiss helped her clear her mind. It didn't have to be all or nothing, but she would have to tell him about

Chris eventually.

"Where are we going tonight?" she asked, when he pulled away.

She felt his gaze on her face. "What are you talking about?"

"You asked me out on a date, remember?" She rolled her head so that she could see him.

He frowned. "But that invitation doesn't stand anymore."

For a moment she felt hurt until she remembered her earlier words about lunch. Just as she was about to smile, his rumbling laughter filled her ears.

She felt the blood drain from her face. Her hands turned icy, and she froze. That laugh belonged to one person and one person only.

Chris.

THOMAS TRIED TO figure what he had done wrong while he waited on Alyssa to get ready for their date. He sat downstairs with a casual arm draped over her couch and flipped the television channels until he felt like he was going cross-eyed.

Alyssa had become quiet and withdrawn. She had made some sort of an excuse to come inside, and just when he thought he was about to get the boot, she turned to him with a brilliantly fake smile and announced she was going to get ready for their date.

Just when he thought the sassy Alyssa was back, the insecure one resurfaced once more.

Thomas sighed and rolled his neck, trying to ease the tension. No wonder people complained about relationships all the time. He sensed she was hiding something. If she'd just tell him what it was, it might actually make things easier. But who was he to tell a divorced woman to just open up to him? He was sure it took courage to start dating again, let alone trust him to stay downstairs while she was taking a shower.

He tried unsuccessfully to stop the visions of water droplets trailing down her body. Her voice drifted to him, a canny and distant sound, but lovely nonetheless. He couldn't tell what she was singing, but just sitting there, remote in hand and woman upstairs, made him feel domestic. Funny how, before today, he wouldn't have admitted to wanting that kind of thing. But all of a sudden, in ways he didn't comprehend, he knew it was meant to be.

His heart lurched at the idea of marriage. But it was too early to tell if he loved Alyssa. Thomas wasn't even sure he was capable of love. With no memories of his past, love seemed like a distant concept to his muddled brain. Love scared him, but at the same time, intrigued him.

He heard the sound of her blow dryer and after a few more minutes, her soft footsteps on the carpeted stairs alerted him to her arrival. Switching off the television, he stood. When she rounded the corner, smiling as always, he did a double take.

Her hair was flowing around her face, an exotic display of waves and fire. Dragging in a breath of air, he saw she wore jeans with high-heeled white sandals, much like the night he first met her at the pool hall. Her shirt was a modest and flowing baby blue, sleeveless button-up that did nothing for her figure but everything for his imagination. His hands itched to feel her.

"Ready?" she asked in a breathy whisper.

All he could do was nod. He stepped toward her, unsure if he should kiss or hug her. He felt the need to give her something, like flowers or chocolate or something equally corny. But what? With a quick glance over to the glass of flowers he brought her earlier in the week, he made a mental note to cut some more for her since they were her favorites. Maybe even buy her a pretty vase.

She didn't say much on the car ride to the theater over

a half hour away. He wanted to ask her if he had done something wrong during their picnic or frightened her somehow, but words escaped him. He did, however, reach for her hand and was happy when she entwined their fingers together and gave him a small squeeze. Trailing his thumb over her soft skin, a sense of peace settled over him. When she was ready, she'd confide in him.

They arrived to a jam-packed theater with a horde of loud teenagers, and Thomas remembered it was Friday. He groaned, hating the weekend scene, but if he wanted to court Alyssa, he would do it the way any other man would. Otherwise, she would feel like she was missing out on something. He doubted the ex even bothered taking her to a movie.

Their hands still together, they walked to the ticket booth, and Thomas took out his wallet. He heard an obnoxious teenager yell something about a freak and tried to focus on Alyssa's smell and the feel of her soft body leaning gently against his as he paid the cashier. He did *not* want to lose his temper in front of her. She'd probably seen enough of that in her lifetime. He glanced back from where the noise came from and saw a group of kids, no older than sixteen, pointing and whispering.

Wasn't this the way things always went for him? His blood pressure rose; he could feel it. He didn't know why kids, and even adults occasionally, felt the need to criticize him for a scar. Was he that horrific? Were they so perfect that they had a free pass to make fun of people less fortunate?

A quick glance into the reflection of the glass in front of him told him yes, it was all that and more. Clenching his jaw, he tugged Alyssa a little too forcefully, and she stumbled. Her searching blue gaze studied his face, and he felt like she was scrutinizing him the same way he always did himself.

He mumbled his apology and pulled her along behind him. "Dude! Look at that hot girl he's got! Betcha he's gotta big one if a woman that pretty sticks around!"

Alyssa jerked away from Thomas before he could grab her. She got in the kid's face, who was looking scared in the storm of her fury. "Don't you dare talk like that about someone you know nothing about."

"Alyssa..." Thomas grabbed her hips, trying to pull her away and keep her from making a scene, but she pushed his hands away.

"Where's your mother?" she demanded. "If she was half decent, she would have taught you that kind of language is unacceptable."

"I don't need you to fight my battles for me," Thomas said in her ear, giving the teenage boy a death glare and wishing once again his life was different.

"Well, someone needs to!" she said, turning her anger on him. "You just stood there and took it."

"Because it's not worth it. He's a kid," he said, pulling her away again. His anger deflated into annoyance.

Before he could open the door, she spun around to the boy again. She got right in his face again and gave a shameful, motherly glare. He was surprised the kid stood his ground. He might have been tempted to walk away himself if she turned that look on him. "I'm not surprised there's no girl here with you."

The smirks of the kid's friends made Thomas grin, but it didn't stop him from feeling irritated at Alyssa for causing such a scene. Everyone was staring.

"Was that really necessary?" he asked, putting his arm around her shoulders after they entered the theater. "He was just a kid. Probably no more than fifteen or sixteen."

"I hate it when teens act like children," she said simply. "I'm a teacher, remember?" Alyssa seemed to have calmed down, but Thomas wasn't sure he could say the same for himself. He couldn't go on if this was how it was going to be every time someone said something. It didn't do much for his ego for a woman half his size to speak up for him.

"I hate that a whit of a woman deems it necessary to fight my battles."

She shrugged off his arm and took a step back, glaring at him. "You're mad at me?" she asked incredulously.

"I'm not pleased, no."

"Well, get over it!"

"What makes your attitude any better than his?" Thomas crossed his arms as the swarms of movie goers walked around them, some obviously listening to their conversation and waiting for the blow up.

Alyssa's mouth moved like a fish out of water, but no sound came out. Still in a tizzy, she snatched the tickets away from him and led the way, practically marching. He watched her cute behind swaying in those jeans.

Shaking his head, he followed her and forced himself to calm down.

AS THEY FILED out of the theater, Thomas kept his eyes peeled for the teenager again, whom he thought he had spotted in the movie. By the time they walked outside and he was in his truck, Thomas had worked himself into a temper.

"If you can't handle the kind of life being with me is going to entail, then you need to get out now."

Alyssa eyed the parking lot and then him with round eyes.

"Metaphorically."

"Are we back to this?" she frowned, crossing her legs and looking away.

"Yes, we are. I'm not kidding. This sort of thing happens all the time, Alyssa. It's nothing new."

Her eyes trained on the car parked next to them, she said, "It's new to me, and it's gotta suck for you."

Thomas exhaled. "I don't pretend to like it. I was thinking of fun ways to make him scream like a girl when you piped up."

She said nothing.

"I appreciate you trying to help me, I really do." He touched her leg and squeezed, trying to get her attention.

"I don't know how you deal with this kind of thing every day." Her voice was suspiciously wobbly and a shot of panic hit Thomas in the gut. He didn't want her pity.

"I don't usually deal with it. I keep to myself unless I go to the pool hall at night. Most everyone there knows me by now, so they've stopped staring."

Alyssa's shocked, tearful gaze riveted to his face. "You did this just for me?"

Thomas swallowed. *Oh no.* "Yes."

She was shaking her head the second he finished speaking. "If this is what happens every time you get out, and you're more comfortable staying in and renting a movie or something, we'll do that instead."

This time he was shaking his head about half way through her suggestion. "No. I will *not* keep you hidden, too. You're giving up plenty to be with me. Tonight was only a small glimpse."

"I don't care, Thomas."

"You will." Of this, he was certain.

"You think I'm that shallow?" Her teary gaze turned angry, and she pushed at his hand. Stubbornly, he refused to move it. "What have I done to deserve such low opinions from the men in my life?"

"I just think you're getting in over your head with me." "Then why don't you stop thinking?"

"Because someone has to be rational here."

"Stop touching me," she hissed. Her hands continued pushing at his. "And you're not being rational."

"Yes, I am being rational. I think your ex did more damage than you think he did. You see me as a safe zone."

The fight went out of her, and she gaped at him. "What?"

"You see me as a safe zone. The scarred-up monster who'll never touch you because I'm afraid you'll leave."

Tears filled her eyes again. "I do *not* see you that way."

"Don't you?"

"No, I don't." The sound of her voice was flat, almost scary in its intensity.

"How do you see me?"

She swiped at her eyes and then settled her gaze back to his. "When I look at you, Thomas, I don't see the scars. I mean, I know they're there. But I see who you are on the inside. When I look past all that anger and pain, I see how scared you are—"

"Oh great," he said, rolling his eyes and looking away. Her tender touch on his scarred cheek urged him to face her.

"I see how brave you are and—"

"How can I be brave and scared at the same time?" he countered, casting his annoyance in her direction.

"That's the very definition of bravery. Facing something you're scared of and not backing down. You can be brave and go through the things you know will be difficult, like surgery, dating, and even the movies. You can be scared because you don't know what will find you each day."

Thomas closed his eyes and thought about his unknown past and how he still waited every day for it to find him. He was definitely scared one day it might.

"I also see how much you want to be loved and how much you want to love someone else, but you use your scars as an excuse."

"No, I don't."

"Yes, you do. You're trying to scare me away before I really even know you. And you're scared that I'm not scared yet."

"I'm awfully scared, huh?"

She grinned and hooked her fingers around his neck,

bringing him over for a chaste kiss. "Why don't you just relax and let this happen, Thomas?"

"Why don't you go out and find someone worth it?"

"Shut up, okay?"

This time, he grinned. "But you know what?"

"What?"

"I've got a pretty big one that makes up for these scars." Alyssa threw her head back and laughed so hard he eventually saw those unshed tears slide down her face. Without thinking too much, he finally let loose and laughed with her. Before long he realized he was the only one laughing. He opened his eyes and settled them on Alyssa.

She sat on her side of the truck, looking at him like he was a ghost. He sobered quickly.

"What's wrong?"

As if she snapped out of a trance, she smiled the fake smile again and shook her head. "Nothing. I just love hearing you laugh. It's not a sound I've heard much of since we've been seeing each other."

He didn't buy it for a second. "Why don't you tell me what you're really thinking?"

His words made her do a double take. "What are you talking about? I mean it. I love hearing you laugh."

Did Thomas believe it? He centered his gaze on her. When he looked at her, he saw a softness he'd never seen there before. Outwardly, she held herself still and cautious. What on earth was going on with her?

He shifted in his seat, trying to figure out how to broach the subject. He realized they were still sitting in the parking lot at the theater and watched as a carefree teenage couple walked together, hand in hand. The boy kissed the girl just before she slipped inside his little sports car.

It was all he could do not to envy those kids.

"Alyssa," he began. "I'm just going to be honest and tell you I know there's something you're hiding from me."

At his words, her face paled, and she bit her lip. "Go on. Tell me whatever it is you know."

Thomas shook his head. "I don't know anything except you're keeping something secret. If I haven't earned your trust yet, I understand. But when you're ready, I hope you'll open up to me."

She stared at him for so long he felt like she had turned to stone. He finally cleared his throat, put the car into gear and drove them home.

Wasn't the beginning of relationships supposed to be like the boy and girl getting into the sports car? Wasn't it supposed to be all hand holding and stolen kisses?

He almost snorted. Maybe if he were sixteen. He didn't even remember twenty, much less his teenage years.

The darkened sky surrounded them. It was almost ten o'clock. He parked in front of Alyssa's house and walked around the car to open her door. Just as he did so, he looked up at the sky and saw the stars winking down at him. He took Alyssa's hand and pulled her out of the car, pointing up into the dim moonlight.

"Gorgeous night," he whispered, keeping her hand in his and pressing his forehead to hers.

"Mmm." She closed her eyes and smiled softly.

He pulled back and lifted her chin so she was forced to look at him. "Listen, I don't want you to think I'm trying to push you into telling me anything. I understand more than anyone the need to be private and keep your secrets. And if it makes you feel any better, I haven't been completely honest with you, either."

Her big blue eyes peered up at him, rounded with curiosity. "I have faith that, with time, everything will make more sense. For both of us."

She nodded. "Me, too."

"You're getting over a pretty rotten breakup, and I've obviously got some issues," he said, pointing to his face. "But I like your advice best. Let's just let this happen."

He grinned as Alyssa trailed her finger down his jaw, her eyes settling on his mouth. "Sounds like a plan."

With that, he cleared his mind of the troubles they were sure to face and kissed her softly, showing her without words all the tenderness filling him up inside.

Chapter Seven

ALYSSA WAS IN her front yard, weeding the flower beds when she heard a car rolling into her driveway. Expecting it to be Thomas, she smiled. They might not have had the best first date ever, but the ending certainly justified the trouble with the teenager.

Renewed with purpose, Alyssa stood, removing her gloves and brushing the dirt off her knees.

"Alyssa."

She turned and saw Jeff standing there, looking ill at ease and more than a little scared of her. Stunned at his arrival, especially since she lived more than two hours away from their hometown, she held her breath, knowing his reasons for coming must be important.

"I wanted to see you." He took his hat from his head and moved it from hand to hand.

She didn't know what to say or do. She made it clear to him on more than one occasion she wasn't interested. She didn't love him the way he wanted her to love him. She never would.

"What's this about?"

Jeff looked away. He wore cowboy boots on his feet and a button up shirt pressed to perfection. That's the way Jeff always looked. Handsome and crisp.

"Well?" she prodded.

"I don't know, Alyssa. I just thought after our last conversation it was time I came back."

She stared at him for a timeless moment. He wasn't acting like himself and hadn't since they'd come to this small town. "Why don't you come inside, and we can talk."

Jeff followed her, his boots tapping a sharp report against the wooden planks on the porch. Inside, Alyssa took a moment to calm her racing heart. She poured lemonade, and they finally settled across from each other at her kitchen table.

"What's this about?" she asked again.

He swallowed but kept a stoic face. "Where are you on your search?"

It was Alyssa's turn to shrug. "Not any further since we spoke last. And I'm thinking about taking your advice and moving on. I still want to continue the search, but I think after five years, I need to think about myself for a little while."

"All of this because you feel sorry for that guy at the bar?" Jeff's his eyes remained on hers, searching and intense.

"I don't feel sorry for him. As a matter of fact, he's really great. Someone I can see myself with. Are you forgetting this was your idea anyway?"

"My idea?" He touched his chest in disbelief.

"You told me to move on. But you didn't mean with anyone else, did you?" Alyssa tried to roll the tension from her shoulders but only succeeded in irritating herself further.

Jeff shifted in his seat and fiddled with the salt shaker in front of him, averting his eyes. "It's not like that, Alyssa. It shocks me a little that you've rented a house and gotten so serious with a guy you've only known for a few weeks."

Alyssa sighed, and he held his hands up in defense.

"I'm on *your* side, okay? I want you to be happy, and if he makes you happy then I'll even come to the wedding. I think I've come to rely on you being a part of my life, and I'm not sure what to do now that you're not. I'm not proud of that, Alyssa. It's not good for my ego to feel like this."

Their eyes met, and Alyssa read the sincerity and shame written in their depths.

"I just want to say I'm sorry. Before I say anything else, I really want you to believe that. I love you, and I believe we could have a great life together, but I understand that you don't feel that way about me. I haven't respected that before, but I do now." He grabbed her hand and squeezed. "Losing Chris has been difficult for me, too. You know, we were friends since grade school, went to high school and college together. Then we opened the business. Having him suddenly disappear really hit me hard."

"I know," Alyssa said, closing her eyes.

"You know how close Chris and I were. But what you don't know is that Chris talked to me a lot about your marriage."

The air left Alyssa's lungs, and she placed her glass on the table with a soft thud and moved away from his touch.

"He never said anything bad. In fact, he always talked about how wonderful you were. That's why it stunned me when he came to me so upset the night he went missing. He told me what happened between you two and what he saw us doing. He didn't give me a chance to explain. He was so angry with himself for letting it happen. That's when he told me he was going to leave for a little while."

Alyssa felt faint. Chris had been gone five years, and Jeff never bothered to tell her this? She knew they had argued and mutually decided to close the business, but not once had Jeff mentioned that Chris had spoken to him again after he left her.

As if reading her mind, he held his hands up. "I

know I should have told you, but it wasn't anything we didn't know. I don't know why I kept it from you, but over time I just thought it was my responsibility to take care of you."

"You wanted to take his place?"

"No! I wanted to make up for what he did to you. I couldn't believe that he could accuse you...accuse *us* of being together, much less just leave you without a trace."

"So you think he's living it up somewhere on a beach with a harem of women living the free life?"

Jeff shook his head. "I don't know what I think."

Needing something to do, Alyssa stood and refilled their glasses. "You might want to keep talking. Chris told me you admitted to having feelings for me. That probably didn't help his stress."

Jeff stood and walked over to her, his expensive cologne filling her nostrils. He leaned against the counter but kept a respectable distance.

"This isn't about that night. I think you need to find out where this guy has been, Alyssa. I just don't have a good feeling about him."

Alyssa's eyes snapped to his. "Why?"

"I don't want you to fill the void and try to replace Chris with this guy."

"You've already told me all of this, Jeff. Why are you really here?" She moved past him and frowned. "And don't think I didn't notice you avoiding my question."

"Same reason I always come back. To protect you."

"I don't need your protection," she spat over her shoulder.

"Listen," he said softly, coming up behind her and placing his hand on her shoulder. "I don't want to tell you how to live your life. It's not why I'm here. I just want to make sure you're okay. Thinking clearly and all that."

Alyssa turned and glared at him. "This is getting old. You've changed since I came here. I don't know if you feel threatened or replaced, but it's time you face the facts. I'm so grateful for all the years you stuck by me and all the things you've done to help me find Chris. But it's not you I want to be with."

After a long sigh, Jeff spoke. "I guess I should be going. I've seen for myself you're okay. I'll leave you alone." Jeff turned and stalked out onto her porch.

"Jeff," she called out as he stepped outside. He turned, looking expectant.

"I don't want to lose you as a friend. But if it's too hard on you, I understand."

Jeff took a step toward her, his gaze riveted to her mouth as she spoke. Uneasiness settled in the pit of her stomach.

"You're beautiful," he whispered, lifting a strand of her hair and playing with it.

"Have you heard anything I've said today?"

"I have," he nodded, looking away. His Adam's apple bobbed as he swallowed. "I'm sorry."

Alyssa didn't know what to think or feel. All she did know was she was overwhelmed. Tears sprang into her eyes and spilled down her cheeks. Jeff's arms came around her, and he tried to comfort her, but his touch felt wrong. At that moment, she only wanted the comfort Thomas could give her. She wanted to feel cherished, not like she was some prize at a carnival. Moving her hands and looking up at Jeff, she read his sorrow and pain, but she didn't care. She placed her hands on his chest and shoved as hard as she could.

"Leave me alone!"

When she shoved him, Jeff fell back and went sliding across the planks of the porch. It was then she noted the movement out of the corner of her eye, and before she registered what was happening, Thomas was there. He yanked Jeff up from the floor and his fist landed against his jaw with a sickening crunch. Jeff barely had time to register the punch before he sprawled back on the porch and received a swift kick in the gut.

"Thomas, no!" Alyssa grabbed his arm and pulled with all her might. The rage she saw on Thomas's face scared her. She feared what he might do if she let him continue. "Stop!" she yelled again. Jeff was crawling backward, trying to get out of his reach.

Thomas didn't seem to register anything until Alyssa grabbed his face and made him look at her.

"Is this the jerk who was stupid enough to divorce you?" His breath came in short, exaggerated puffs as he spoke through clenched teeth.

"No, Thomas. Jeff and I have never been married." Alyssa didn't remove her hands from his shoulders, just to ensure he didn't feel the need to punch Jeff again.

"Then who is this joker? I recognize him from the bar the first night I saw you. Surely there's something going on between you two."

Alyssa glanced at Jeff. "Nothing is going on between us and never will. I realized today who really has my heart."

Thomas looked at her, and his face softened a little. His eyes strayed back to Jeff. "Get in your car and go home," he said through clenched teeth. Thomas pulled Alyssa into the safe haven of his arms and placed a gentle hand on the back of her head, urging her to rest against him.

Jeff scurried to a standing position beside them. She felt the heat of his body as he got into Thomas's face. Peering upward, she saw Jeff's sneer and the ugly bruise forming on his jaw.

"Some things never change," he hissed.

Confused by his words, Alyssa felt the guilt weighing heavily on her shoulders when she heard Jeff's vehicle start up and back out of her driveway. Thomas's hold on her tightened, and he planted a soft kiss on the top of her head. After a moment, he pulled back and put a gentle hand on her cheek, looking deeply into her eyes.

"Are you okay?" he asked.

Alyssa smiled. "I'm fine."

"I'm never going to let anyone hurt you again, do you understand me?" he said, earnestness in his voice and a plea in his eyes. His mouth was set in a determined line, and she knew he meant every word.

Alyssa's heart broke into a million pieces then, just looking at Thomas. Bringing his head down for a kiss, she closed her eyes and allowed herself to really let go for the first time in years. This man, with the face of a stranger, could be anyone, and she'd still feel the same way.

His mouth worked over hers, confident and soft, and she felt her body responding to him. There was no question in her mind when they reached the level of intimacy she longed for it would be amazing.

The tears on her face surprised her. Everything that just transpired with Jeff was too much. She hadn't digested the information and feared she was riding on an emotional wave destined to crash. Wrenching away from Thomas, she swept the tears away from her cheeks. Thomas looked at her with a worried frown.

"I think I just need to be alone for a little while," Alyssa whispered. Actually, it was the last thing she wanted, but it was necessary.

He released her. "I'll be here to pick up the pieces when you're ready, Alyssa. I know it's not easy losing the people you love most."

She smiled and took his hands in hers. "The pieces are back together and healing quite nicely. Thanks to you," she whispered and kissed him again. "You have my heart, Thomas. What's left of it."

Alyssa meant it. Regardless of Jeff's feelings, Thomas was the man she wanted to move forward with.

Thomas looked uncomfortable at her declaration, but he gave her a lopsided grin. "That makes me happy." He pulled her into his arms for a quick hug. "Call me when you want some company."

As he walked away, she called, "Why did you stop by

anyway?"

He turned, walking backward and shrugged. "Doesn't matter."

She propped her hands on her hips. "Tell me."

"I was going to see if you wanted to come with me to my surgeon's appointment tomorrow. It's a little bit of a drive, but it's a great city. I thought we could stick around and do something afterward."

She smiled. "I'd love to."

He frowned. "Are you sure?"

"Absolutely."

He nodded once. "Then I'll pick you up at nine in the morning." She tossed him a wave as he left, a myriad of feelings flowing through her. Despite her best efforts to reconcile Jeff's parting words, she was more frustrated than ever that she simply couldn't decide whether to keep moving forward with Thomas, or stay in the past searching for Chris.

Saddened and confused, Alyssa went inside to work through her emotions.

THOMAS PACED THE wooden floor of his bedroom, trying to figure out why he was so antsy. Alyssa said the guy never laid a hand on her. But did he believe her? Yes, he did, but when he'd happened upon the argument, he hadn't liked what he heard.

What didn't jive with him was how she seemed unsure about being with him. Sure, she argued when he voiced his concerns, but his gut told him there was more to it than that. She even admitted to him that her heart wasn't whole anymore.

Thomas sat on the edge of his bed and ran his hand over his face. A deep breath calmed him some until it dawned on him why he couldn't settle down. He was jealous.

Rolling his eyes, he tried to shrug it off, chalking it up to the fact Alyssa was the first relationship he could remember having. He didn't want to be jealous. Alyssa had made it clear she didn't know what she wanted from him from the beginning, and he had no claims. There were no promises between them.

She'd specifically said tonight he had her heart. So how could he have her heart when she still thought she couldn't have what she wanted?

Tired, Thomas decided it was best to quit over-analyzing. He lived his life day-to-day and although he loved being with Alyssa, he couldn't let things run away with him and start thinking long-term. If she decided she wanted the guy on her porch that was her prerogative. If she wanted her ex back, who was he to stop her? Thomas knew it was a slim chance she'd choose him anyway.

Gritting his teeth, he decided he just couldn't let it matter.

SHE WALKED TOWARD him like perfection, dressed in white. The thick veil preceded her, obscuring a clear view of her face. Thomas saw the wavy, red hair flowing behind the veil and the color flagged something in his brain as familiar. When she reached him, she took his hand and squeezed tightly.

He smiled at her even though he couldn't really see her. His eyes narrowed in a squint, trying to gaze past the haze the veil created.

"Are you nervous?" she whispered, her voice satiny smooth in his ear. A thumb traced circles against his skin.

"How could I be nervous when I'm about to have every-thing I've ever wanted?" He felt his cheeks rise in a full smile, the movement feeling awkward. "I love you."

"I love you, too. Let's do this."

Eagerly he nodded and turned. He saw the minister stand-ing there, giving them a quick smile. After he cleared his throat, he began speaking, uniting their love and their life in only a few moments. Thomas's heart thumped against his chest, an unknown feeling filling him up.

"You may kiss the bride," the minister said and motioned for them to come together.

Carefully, Thomas grasped the bottom of the veil and pulled it up. Focused on making sure there were no wrinkles, he smoothed the fabric and finally turned his eye to his bride. His heart lurched when he saw that he only moved a portion of the veil. He raised the rest of it up with a grin, thinking about how everyone would laugh.

But there was more. And even more. He threw the part in his hand over her head. He tugged uselessly for the headdress to come free of her hair. Frantically, he searched for the end of the insanity, but every time he thought he got it all, he would look back where his bride's face was supposed to be and all that was there was the distorted image behind a veil that he couldn't clear up.

Taking a step back, Thomas realized within his dream that something was wrong. He should be able to see her, touch her. A wedding was the one time everything was supposed to be perfect.

Only it wasn't.

STILL HALF ASLEEP, Thomas's eyes shot open. His body was lined with sweat, and he felt paralyzed with fear. What was he supposed to make of that?

Pushing past the gripping fear of the dream, he sat up and ran his palm over his face. The sheet slid down his bare chest and puddled around his waist. He felt so lost when he had dreams like this.

Murphy's head rose from where he slept on the floor at Thomas's groan, but he quickly dismissed the movement and settled his head down to continue sleeping. This wasn't the first time Thomas experienced dreams that didn't make any sense. There were dreams where he was lost and couldn't find anyone to show him the way home. Only an expanse of flowers surrounded him with no end in sight.

Then there was the dream of the older woman, much like a doting and loving mother, whose face wilted in the light of a blinding sun.

He was pathetic. He wasn't sure who he was kidding more, Alyssa or himself, if he thought he could offer her any form of a normal life. With the resurfacing of these dreams lately, Thomas admitted to himself something he knew was inevitable from the moment he first met Alyssa.

It was time to tell her the truth.

It was time to tell her he had no past, no family, no memory and, quite possibly, no future. She was his now, his present.

He often imagined a grand reunion between him and a family. One look and all of his memories would come flooding back, impossible as it was. He envisioned a loving wife, maybe a kid or two, and his life would no longer be in limbo. He could start living.

Now, he prayed no family or wife existed. If there was, it would only complicate things. He prayed whoever might know him, wife or otherwise, had moved on.

As far as he was concerned, *everything* with Alyssa was riding on his next surgery. He would stress the importance to his doctor that things had to be done right. There was a reason to live now, a reason to hope. With that thought came a realization Thomas hadn't wanted to acknowledge.

He was falling in love with Alyssa Morgan.

Chapter Eight

"SO WHAT IS your doctor's appointment for?" Alyssa asked as she crawled into Thomas's truck, looking beautiful as ever. Her wavy hair fell loose around her shoulders, and she wore a button-up pink blouse and dark jeans. On her feet were shiny brown pumps.

"You look good enough to eat," Thomas teased and leaned in for a kiss.

She met him half way with a grin playing on her mouth. It was a sweet joining, but Thomas's need accelerated to feverish levels. His dream last night left him with an urgency he didn't realize he possessed. He grabbed the back of her head and pushed closer, but she broke away, brushing his lips and laughing a little.

"Beige shimmer isn't your color."

"It could be purple for all I care right now."

"You'll care when your doctor thinks you're there for a sex change."

Thomas couldn't help it; he threw his head back and laughed harder than he had in a long time. "Something tells me my doctor knows me a little better than that."

"I hope so." She shook her head. "So what's this appointment for?"

"It's my pre-op consult. I'm having surgery in a few days."

"What for?"

He admonished her with a look. "What do you think?"

"Your scars?"

Her worried frown touched him, but it also brought to light all the complications his surgery might cause. The constant pain, the physical therapy, having to be waited on hand and foot for a few weeks was only the beginning.

"Yes."

"I thought you said you already had surgery."

"I did, but I have to have at least two more. The surgeon has to reconstruct my face one surgery at a time to allow new skin to grow. Each one builds on itself. My new face won't be complete for another four years." He backed out of the driveway and they were on their way.

"So this is your second surgery?"

He shook his head. "Fourth. They did the first surgery when I got to the hospital, a second one a year later. Then I had another one the third year and now this one five years later."

"Is there a lot of pain afterward?"

Thomas shrugged, hoping all the information didn't make Alyssa feel sorry for him any more than she already did. "I'll be doped up on pain killers for about two weeks, so in your spare time you'll have to take care of me. You know, give me a sponge bath and such." He angled a wink at her, and she giggled.

"Something tells me this surgery has nothing to do with your ability to bathe." She was grinning, and he couldn't help but return it.

"I really will be out of it for about two weeks."

Alyssa took his hand and squeezed. "I'll be here to help you."

He smiled. "Good. That's all I can ask for."

She grew pensive for a little while, looking out her window. When she turned back to him, she looked troubled. "Who helped you during your first three surgeries?"

Thomas shook his head. "Nobody really. My boss dropped in a few times to bring dinner and make sure I was okay, but mostly it was just me and a bottle of heavy duty pain killers."

"I'm sorry, Thomas," she whispered. "I wish I could have been here for you."

"Five years ago, you were with your ex. You wouldn't have been able to do much for me with him around. At least, not what I would have had in mind." He gave her his best grin.

"I would have found a way." The way she studied him unnerved him. It reminded him of the way she had looked at him that night at the bar.

"Speaking of your ex, when are you going to tell me the whole story?"

He saw her swallow out of the corner of his eye. She looked nervous all of a sudden.

"You know, if we're going to have what most would consider a real relationship, you need to tell me everything." He was one to talk wasn't he? But he hoped this would open up a window of opportunity for him to bring up his own past.

"I've told you everything I know, Thomas. What more do you want?" But the telltale way she fiddled with the zipper on her purse told him she wasn't being totally honest.

"The truth. I know he hit you."

Her head snapped in his direction. "No, actually he didn't...But he did hurt me by accusing me of cheating."

"Did you?"

"Never."

"How long ago was it?"

She swallowed again when he glanced at her. "A little over five years ago."

He mulled over that information. Each moment during the same five years led them to each other. Thomas couldn't help but be glad. "I guess we have that in common then, huh? We could have helped each other heal back then. We should have just saved ourselves the trouble and found each other first, right?" Thomas's heart ached over the fact Alyssa had been alone as long as he had. But now a different thought burned on his tongue.

"Fate has a way of bringing people together when it's the right time," Alyssa said. "Back then, I don't think he would have been receptive to the truth. He was going through a lot."

"You must have really loved him to not be over him five years later."

Alyssa pulled her hand away from his and looked out the window as the houses and trees passed by. "I loved him a lot, Thomas. But I've given it a lot of thought, and I'm ready. I want a future with you."

Her eyes met his momentarily before she looked back to the road. How had his luck changed this way? Through Alyssa's earnestness, he knew she spoke the truth. But was it fair for her to lay it all on the line and him not give anything back? Strangely, he believed her now when she said her ex hadn't hit her.

How would she react to the fact he was a John Doe? Did he want to see what her eyes said then?

"Alyssa, I think I need to tell you something," he began with his heart in his throat. This could change everything. He could lose her before he ever really had a chance.

"What is it?" She tried to take his hand again, but he couldn't stand the thought of her tender caress when she might demand he turn the car around once he was through. He switched hands on the steering wheel before she could touch him.

"I haven't told you much about my past, you know?"

"I just thought it was painful for you to talk about. I can't imagine all you've been through."

"It is difficult to talk about, mainly because…"

"Go on."

Thomas let the air out of his lungs in a big whoosh. He was an idiot. *Now* was not the time to tell her about this. But tonight, he vowed, he would, as soon as they got home. He would enjoy this one day with her and forget about it until then. This might be the last day he spent in her company.

"Never mind," he said. "We'll talk about it when we get home tonight."

WHEN DR. LASKA walked in, clad in the typical white lab coat, stethoscope peeking from his hip pocket, and silver-rimmed reading glasses perched on his nose, Alyssa couldn't help but smile. She also smiled at the sight of a shirtless Thomas. Up until now, she hadn't realized his injuries extended to his shoulder, too. When she mentioned it, he said it was mostly superficial, but the scars didn't look to be. They were situated on top of his shoulder, where he skidded across the pavement without protection on his skin.

"Good morning, Thomas. How are you feeling today?" Dr. Laska grabbed his stool and sat down so he was on his patient's level.

Thomas had been unusually quiet after he told Alyssa he wanted to talk to her when they got home. Now was no exception. He gave the doctor a little nod, but otherwise said nothing.

"How have you been feeling?"

Another nod.

"Any pain?"

He shrugged. "A little."

Alyssa's mind wandered back to the night she touched his scars, and he had mentioned the nerve-endings still gave him trouble. Was it possible he was in pain more than he let on? The thought made her heart lurch.

"Short-term memory still good?"

Nod.

"Have you had any long-term memories resurface?" Thomas's eyes rounded and darted between her and the doctor. For the first time, Dr. Laska looked at Alyssa where she stood in the corner of the room. Their words finally came together in her brain, and her heart jumped into her throat. What did he say about memories?

The doctor turned a questioning glance at Thomas, who nodded his approval and looked away from Alyssa. She knew him well enough by now to know shame overwhelmed him.

"No," he said quietly.

A deep breath didn't stop the way her heart beat against her rib cage, desperate to hear more.

"Well," the doctor continued, shining a light in Thomas's eyes. "That's typical for retrograde amnesia. I'm sure your neurologist has explained you may never get your memories back, and if you do, it might be bits and pieces that only confuse you."

Thomas nodded, risking a glance at her. Alyssa couldn't move.

This was a big secret for him to have kept from her for so long.

She sat down in the chair next to her.

The doctor finished his exam, explaining in detail what he would be doing to Thomas's face this time. He used charts and models and explained how skin removed from Thomas's leg would be used to help increase elasticity. It sounded horrific. Alyssa watched Thomas's unwavering gaze as Dr. Laska explained. He didn't grimace or frown. He was the model of patience and gratitude.

"We have you scheduled for this Thursday. We'll get started around ten, so be here no later than eight for pre-op. Nothing to eat or drink after midnight. I'll see you then, Thomas."

Thomas took the man's extended hand and nodded his acceptance. "Thank you. Thursday it is."

"Be sure to drink plenty of fluids between now and

then. No stress and no over-exerting yourself," he re-minded Thomas with a pointed look in Alyssa's direction.

When the door closed, Alyssa sat in stunned silence. She simply didn't know what to say or what to believe anymore. No, she hadn't been truthful with him about why she was here, but it didn't seem to matter now. She wanted Thomas in her life, but did the amnesia change anything? Alyssa didn't think so, but what if there was another woman out there waiting for him like she had waited for Chris for so long?

Quietly, Thomas spoke first. "I was going to tell you in the car, but it didn't seem to be the right time."

"Amnesia?" she choked, tears filling her eyes.

"Yeah. Apparently I've lost my mind."

Alyssa stood, angrier than she could remember being in a long time. "This isn't a joke, Thomas. This is your life!"

He closed his eyes slowly, biting his lower lip. "I'm sorry."

"What about your family or friends? Surely someone helped you through this."

"If I have family or friends, they never bothered to look for me."

The statement was issued so vehemently Alyssa reeled back. "Did *you* look for *them*?"

"Kind of hard to look for people you don't remember." He had a point.

"What did you do?"

"Nothing."

"Nothing?" Alyssa practically yelled and took a step closer.

"My boss was the one who found me. He offered to search out my family after it was clear no one was looking for me, but I told him I'd rather not. If they don't want me, I don't want them."

Alyssa found it ironic she had been looking for a man who didn't want to be found, yet here was Thomas, in a similar predicament who obviously wanted a family, even if he didn't know it.

"A real friend would have searched for them anyway, instead of letting you roll in self-pity," Alyssa pointed out, poking an angry finger at his bare chest.

Thomas's jaw pulsed with irritation. "He's the only friend I have, Alyssa. He's the only one who cared enough to look past all of this and give me a chance." He watched her closely as he slid off the paper-covered examination table.

"I've looked past it. Give me a little credit here." She shook her head, trying to clear her muddled brain.

"Yes, you've looked past it. For now. I guess we'll see about later."

Alyssa straightened her back and nodded. She recognized his words for the challenge they were. "Why didn't you tell me sooner?"

He shrugged and turned his back to her, bending to get his shirt. "Same reason you haven't told me everything yet."

Something caught her eye as he stood erect and pulled his shirt over his head.

Alyssa knew the true meaning of feeling paralyzed. There, right where it was supposed to be, just to the left of his right shoulder blade was a heart shaped freckle she and Chris used to laugh over. She couldn't believe she had forgotten about it until now. How many times had she kissed that freckle? How many times had she teased Chris about God giving him a tattoo? She sat down, feeling faint, then she stood up again, her body trembling. No. It was just a similar mark. There was no way Thomas could be Chris. There was no way she had been with him this long and not known her husband's touch.

Alyssa blinked to clear her eyes and looked again. It was still there. A little heart with another freckle just above it, positioned like the moon was to the earth.

Stumbling, she grabbed the edge of the counter. Ignoring Thomas's worried frown, she walked over to him, wrapped her arms around his neck, unable to hold back the sobs that wracked her body. Immediately, Thomas pulled her into his arms with a sigh and held her tightly. Quietly, he shushed her, smoothed her hair and placed kisses against her temple.

Dismissing her initial instincts that Thomas was Chris seemed absurd now. She should have told him from the very beginning who she was and why she was so interested. What precious time they had wasted!

The full impact of all Thomas went through hit her harder than ever. He had spent so much time alone and hurting. She hadn't been looking hard enough. But when all the layers were stripped away and everything was laid bare, she realized now this whole time she was expecting him to be dead. And to know how close that expectation had come to a reality...

But here he was, holding her, touching her. Breathing. *Alive.*

She tightened her hold on him.

God, she prayed and closed her eyes, *don't let me mess this up. Let me get him back.* Thomas scooped her into his arms and sat on the small chair in the room.

Now that she knew Chris was alive, she wasn't sure what to do. Did she tell him? Did she wait until the right moment? But she remembered the animosity in his voice at the mention of his family and knew the smarter choice would be to ease him into it. He was right to feel abandoned and helping him realize things would be different now wouldn't be an easy task.

When she first met Thomas, anger emanated from him like a red-hot ember ready to burst into flames. Now that she knew him, she realized how much more there was inside of him, but it was a thin line to walk to keep him from going back into his shell.

"You're shaking, Alyssa. Are you okay? Do you need me to get the doctor? I knew I shouldn't have sprung this on you like this." His concerned voice penetrated through her thoughts. She pulled back, shaking her head. His voice. How could she forget that voice?

"No, I'm okay. I'm more than okay." His brows rose. "No, you're not."

She laughed, shakily. "I'm just so glad you're okay. When I think about what could have happened. It could have been so much worse than just losing your memory." Collapsing into tears again, she pressed her lips to his in a gentle kiss.

"If you want me to be honest, there were days I wish I *had* died. It might have been easier." He wiped away her tears and gave her a tender smile. "But now I'm glad I didn't."

Alyssa gave him another hug and then released him. "Let's get out of here."

As he unfolded his arms and released her, Alyssa stole another glance at the freckle. There was no denying it was exactly what she remembered.

Her life would never be the same again.

Then again, neither would his.

"I'VE HEARD OF this neat little place downtown with great food and dancing. What do you think about that?" Thomas asked Alyssa as they left the physician's office. She hadn't released his hand except for when she got in his truck. Now that he was sitting next to her again, her hand went to his.

It was a sweet, yet possessive gesture, one that Thomas enjoyed. He had foolishly thought telling her of his amnesia would change things. If there was one thing he knew about Alyssa during their short acquaintance, it was that she was dedicated. When he thought of all the time she wasted on her ex, on a man who had never really appreciated her, he decided he wouldn't waste time. He'd never let her go and spend the rest of his life thanking God for a second chance at life. Maybe he could look forward to the future now.

"That sounds great," Alyssa said with a big smile.

There was something in the way she looked at him since finding out about his amnesia. There was clarity in her eyes and brightness in her smile he hadn't seen before. Were his secrets all that separated them before? Now all he had to do was get her to talk about her skeletons, and they would both be free to move ahead.

The thought made his heart soar.

He took a deep breath and smoothed his thumb over her skin. He licked his lips, speaking hesitantly. "Are you sure you're okay with this? I mean, the amnesia leaves a lot of unanswered questions about my previous life."

She held a hand up to stop him. "I do wish you had told me sooner. A good relationship is founded on trust. But, to be honest, I think we've both made mistakes. We've both kept things from each other. As for your previous life, let's talk about that later, okay? I don't want to think about it right now."

With a solemn nod, he agreed, and they left the parking lot. They spent a few hours walking around an outdoor mall, got ice cream, and ate a quick lunch of hot dogs and relish. They wasted time together until their six o'clock dinner reservation at a restaurant called The Pelican Nest. It was the kind of place Thomas only saw on television.

Black tablecloths covered every table with a single candle lit in the middle. The dim light in the room caused him to squint a little. Cooked seafood met his nostrils. His stomach rolled in anticipation. A soft melody from a live piano lilted through the air, and Thomas couldn't wait to hold Alyssa in his arms again.

The hostess led them to a seat toward the back of the room, but still within viewing distance of the dance floor. As they were seated, Alyssa shot him a wink. He smiled and took her hand as soon as they were situated. Now it was his turn to want to touch her. He felt liberated beyond his wildest expectations. No one except Jerry had known the truth about him—until now. Thomas took a deep, cleansing breath and let it out.

His heart burst with happiness. This woman was responsible for giving him such a freedom he never thought possible.

"I don't know about you," Alyssa whispered, "but I feel a little under dressed."

Thomas eyed her pink shirt and heels and shrugged. "We're giving them money, surely they won't mind. I happen to think you look amazing."

Alyssa gave him a breathtaking smile, and he held his breath. He, Thomas Williams, wasn't the monster he always thought he was. It was within his power to make a beautiful woman smile.

He mulled over these things while they ate and thought about the dramatic turn his life had suddenly taken. How, only months before, his life served no purpose, never thinking past the very moment he was living in because he of all people understood how it could all be taken in the blink of an eye. But the future was all Thomas could think about now; a future with Alyssa and her brilliant smile that filled every dark corner with her sunshine.

"Let's dance," he murmured as he stared at her.

She closed her eyes for a moment as if she was savoring a rich piece of chocolate. With a slow nod, she stood, and he took her hand.

Glancing toward the front door, he saw dusk had fallen. It would be late when they returned home, but the busy, chaotic day was well worth it given the circumstances.

He knew as he looked at Alyssa walking into his arms with such tenderness shining in her eyes, the fall was complete. He was in love with Alyssa Morgan.

The thought didn't scare him as much as he thought it would. Truth be told, he had never expected to be in this position. Now that he was, he was even more grateful for the opportunity. He wouldn't run scared anymore. They hadn't made commitments to each other yet, but Thomas felt it was nearing the time he should bring it up.

Wrapping his arms snugly around her, he lowered his head and inhaled the scent of roses. The smell combined with Alyssa's nearness was intoxicating.

"What are you thinking?" she asked a little while later as they swayed together.

"Mmm," he said with closed eyes and a grin on his face. "You don't want to know."

"Yes, I do."

"Uh-uh. Another time." He placed a kiss in the crook of her neck.

Her fingernails speared through his short hair, sending goose bumps down his spine.

"Not even a little hint?" she whispered huskily in his ear. The tone in her voice was sexy, and his hands dropped to pull her hips against his, answering her question.

"I wouldn't call it little, personally," he rasped.

He felt her smile against his cheek as her hips moved and played against his. He didn't know if dancing like this was a good thing or a bad thing. All he knew is he didn't want to be anywhere else but at the same time would give everything he owned to be back at his house, holding her just like this.

"Definitely not little," she agreed and pulled back to look into his eyes.

The blue of her eyes were emphasized tonight in the candlelight, as was her red hair. "You're beautiful, Alyssa," he said, surprising himself with the intensity of his words.

Her grin was lazy but her eyes held his with an equal fervor.

"So are you," she said.

Thomas looked away and swallowed. He wanted to believe her more than anything, but he saw the ugly truth when he looked in the mirror.

Alyssa's graceful hand pulled his face back to hers. "Would it change anything if I was the one with the scars? Would you see me any different than you do now?"

Thomas was shaking his head before the questions were out. "Not a chance."

"Then what makes it so hard for you believe that I find you attractive?"

He shrugged. "I just want to be everything for you."

Tears welled in her eyes, and she touched his lips with her fingertips. "You already are."

This time, when Thomas looked at her, he saw the truth written in the shimmering tear on her cheek. He felt her urgency in the way she gripped his forearm. He tasted her love as their lips met and caressed.

He would never doubt her again. The spell had broken and he was finally a prince, not a beast.

Alyssa pulled away just enough so she could speak. "Take me home, Thomas. With you."

His hands framed her cheeks and his face furrowed in concentration as he thought about the meaning behind those last two words. Every way he turned them in his mind, they all came back to the same conclusion. "Are you sure, Alyssa?"

Her fingers wrapped around his wrists as her eyes danced back and forth between his. Her nod was all he needed.

Throwing a large wad of cash from his pocket onto their table, he hauled her across the dance floor and out the door. She giggled when he practically threw her into the cab of his truck.

All he could think about as he peeled out of the parking lot a few moments later was how long the drive home would be.

Chapter Nine

THE NIGHT WAS so pretty outside, Alyssa convinced Thomas to roll the windows down and let the cool air in. Nothing felt more exhilarating during the two-hour drive home than feeling nature against her skin and knowing she would soon be feeling Thomas's hands instead.

She watched in amusement as Thomas broke the speed limit by at least ten miles an hour. His hands fisted the steering wheel, and in the darkness she could see the white knuckles from his grasp.

Alyssa wondered why she still thought of him as Thomas, even though there was solid evidence he was Chris. The only explanation she could come up with was the drastic differences between the two men. They might share the same body, but the men inside of it were as different as night and day.

Alyssa had fallen in love with both of them.

Even before seeing that freckle on him, Alyssa had loved Thomas. It hadn't been much of a choice really. Little by little, he had inched into her life, being around or arguing with her, making her feel like she was a part of *his* life. Before she knew it, she couldn't imagine a day, or a week without him. She said a prayer of thanks her first instinct about Thomas led her to stay. She didn't want to think about what could have happened if she had walked away.

She didn't care if Thomas was Chris or Chris was Thomas, she wanted both men. She didn't care which form she got him in as long as he was still hers.

Her husband was alive.

As much as Alyssa could figure, she still thought of the man sitting next to her as Thomas because he *was* Thomas. Chris was a different man and, as sad as it made Alyssa to think she would never have him back in a literal sense, she knew everything would be okay.

The only thing that really bugged her was Thomas would never remember her. She could go on pretending they had just met, but she couldn't do that to him. He was obviously bitter over the whole situation and it was her responsibility to give him some peace of mind.

Retrograde amnesia. Alyssa shook her head, still amazed she had never seen what was right in front of her.

Thomas pulled the truck into his driveway, the crunch of gravel like fireworks in the still night air. Alyssa heard a lone cricket hidden somewhere in the bushes chirp a greeting.

Thomas didn't hesitate to cut the engine off and get out of the car. He opened the door for her and pulled her out, only to pin her against it the second it was shut.

He smiled down at her. "Just a little confession I need but don't want to make...It may be big, but it's neglected. I don't want you to expect much the first go around."

Alyssa couldn't help but giggle. "Don't worry about it."

He cocked an eyebrow at her as the corner of his mouth quirked in amusement.

"I get it, Thomas. Now shut up and kiss me."

"Not out here. We'll never make it to the bed. At least let me get that part right."

She rolled her eyes. "You can be melodramatic, did you know that?"

"Don't ruin the mood for me, okay?" He tugged her

toward the house, and stopped at the front porch to open the door.

"As if I could," she mumbled.

He shot her a pointed look, and she realized for the first time he was nervous. He'd said he hadn't been with anyone since his accident. *Amnesia*. Her breath hitched as he opened the door when she realized what that meant.

"What? Don't tell me you're having second thoughts. If you are, that's just cruel," Thomas said.

"You don't remember ever making love, do you?"

He kept his back to her as they entered the house, but she could hear the note of irritation in his voice. "No."

She knew when he began to speak in one word sentences she would have to pry the truth from him. She decided not to say anything else unless he brought it up. Just because she was figuring out more details didn't mean that he wasn't sick to death of thinking about his situation.

"Welcome to my humble abode," Thomas said and threw his keys down on the kitchen table with a loud clang. Murphy came trotting up to him for a pat but Thomas turned and let him out on the back deck.

"It's nice," Alyssa said. She felt as out of place in his home as his scar looked on his face. She suddenly felt unsure of herself.

He offered her a glass of ice water. She took it but didn't drink. Thomas stood there, across the kitchen and watched her.

Shifting her weight from one foot to another, she wondered what to do next.

"What?" he asked with a trace of irritation still in his voice.

"I'm not sure," she admitted. "I guess I'm just curious." She opted for the truth. "Curious about what?"

She walked over, standing in front of him. "Curious about what parts of you have been affected by your amnesia."

"Everything."

Alyssa reached up and touched his face, trailing her finger down and across his jaw on his good side. She watched as his breathing labored and the pulse in his neck leaped. "I'm curious about what it would feel like to kiss you when I know it won't stop at just a kiss this time."

"By all means."

It was the opening she needed, yet she hesitated to take it. He clearly anticipated her kiss, but he made no move to encourage it. He simply stood there watching her, reminding her of the Thomas she had met at the bar, not the one who she worked so hard to break through to.

Alyssa touched the button of his shirt and twisted it, studying it. Chris had never worn green plaid button-up shirts. He was more of a polo or t-shirt kind of man. She watched Thomas's hand as it moved to her hip and pulled her close. The flutter in her heart caused her to gasp. Desire pooled within her at his touch.

"Are you afraid of me after all?" he whispered against her ear.

The desire turned to fire. He smelled so good.

She turned and placed her head and against his. "You know better than that."

He pulled back just enough so she could feel his breath against her cheek. She was suddenly tired of waiting.

Pressing her lips against his, she remembered those were the lips that belonged to her husband. The lips that once kissed every inch of her. The lips she had waited five years to feel again.

A whimper escaped her, and she threw her arms around Thomas's neck, deepening the kiss. At first he hesitated, but as she pulled him close and kissed him urgently, he warmed up. His tongue swept inside her mouth, a wonderful reminder of all they had lived without for so long. Her body responded to him, and she worked on his buttons blindly. His hands didn't roam. In fact, other than kissing her, he didn't move.

She broke away and smiled at him. "Touch me. I need to feel you touch me." She felt like she was in a whirlwind, unable to get to him fast enough. All she wanted was her husband making love to her. "Touch me," she demanded and looked up at him.

"Don't you think we should slow down?

"I don't want to think, I want to feel. Touch me," she said hoarsely. His sharp intake of breath told her he wasn't as immune to her as he pretended. It had been so long since she felt anything like this. This was what she could never get enough of.

"Alyssa..." he started but enough was enough. For a moment, they stood eye to eye.

His control snapped and his mouth slammed into hers. His hand left her and instead of making pretense with her buttons, he ripped her shirt open and slid it over her shoulders.

Fueled only by their desire, Alyssa's world melted away and it was only the two of them. His lips roamed over her chest. With her fingers spread through his short hair, she pressed her face into his neck and reveled in the perfect feeling of being home. Time was erased. The five years that separated them no longer existed.

Stumbling awkwardly, he caught his balance, holding on to her. She smiled inwardly while outwardly straining against him for everything he was willing to give.

He led her to his bed, which was littered with clothes. Hurriedly he threw everything on the floor and shot her an apologetic look. She smiled at him, happier than she ever remembered being.

Instead of joining her on the bed, he just looked at her and ran his hand down his face, a gesture she remembered Chris doing when frustration ate at him.

"Are you okay?"

His eyes darted away and he shook his head. "I can't do this."

Alyssa frowned. "You can't?" But she had felt his reaction to her on more than one occasion. Surely there wasn't something that had happened to him that prevented him from making love.

Her eyes darted to his pants and back to his scar.

The corner of his lip lifted in an almost-smile. "No, believe me, I'm *capable*. I'm just afraid that I'm a little more traditional than this. This isn't what I envisioned."

"Why don't you tell me what you envisioned?"

"I don't want it to be rushed and out of control."

"Can we negotiate?" she countered thoughtfully.

He just sighed. "The timing isn't right. It's been a long day for both of us. Let's start over tomorrow with a nice dinner."

"Thomas, can we just forget about pretenses? I'm not complicated. I'm pretty simple, actually. I just want to make love to you. Right now."

His mouth quirked, and he took a step toward her. "Are you sure?"

"Yes." Alyssa shot him a big smile and couldn't help her giddy response at his nearness. "As long as you can handle me," she teased. She stood and walked to him, taking his hand in hers.

Chris. Her Chris. She had found him.

Thomas's lips touched hers softly, reverently. When he pulled away, he watched his hand as he pushed her hair away from her face. "There's one more thing I want to say before we do this," he said huskily.

"Don't you think we should stop talking now?"

He grinned but ignored her. "You're the only one who cared enough to stick around when I wasn't very nice to you. That means a lot to me."

Alyssa nodded and wrapped her arms around Thomas's waist, looking up at him. "I knew you were special the second I saw you."

The scrutiny in his eyes turned solemn, and his fingertips traced her lips, studying them intently. His brows were furrowed in concentration, a strained look taking over his features. "I love you, Alyssa," he whispered.

Her heart stopped and then restarted with a great thump against her chest. Surprise stole her breath, and her hands fell from his waist. How lucky that Thomas could come to love her twice in their lifetime. How lucky she could love the man he had become just as much as the man she first fell in love with.

Tears welled in her eyes, and she pressed her lips to his again. Pulling back only enough to speak, she whispered in return, "I love you, too, Thomas."

Gently, his arms encircled her and his hands roamed her back. He walked with her to the bed and followed her down. She didn't need to see his eyes to know her words meant more to him than she could imagine. He lived his life in seclusion until now, so affection wasn't something he was accustomed to. He was remarkably good at it despite that fact.

The weight of his body felt delicious against hers. The urgency from earlier eased into a burning desire no longer born of desperation, but rather patience and happiness. For Thomas, this was something like the first time, and she wanted it to be special.

He kissed her, taking time to do it slowly and thoroughly. Even though he didn't kiss the same way he used to, it was no less wonderful. This was a side to him he had never unleashed; Chris was tender and sweet and while Thomas was, too, she could sense his tightly controlled libido and felt his power against her belly.

Slowly, he trailed his fingers against her skin. When she was lying in front of him, exposed, he leaned his head forward and touched his lips to her neck. She closed her eyes and bit her bottom lip, fighting tears; the sense of homecoming overwhelmed her.

His hands splayed against the expanse of her rib cage, and he trailed kisses across her stomach. He rose and with a look of intense concentration and kissed her deeply, his tongue sweeping deep and low. Alyssa kissed him back, giving all she could, trying to convey her feelings in a single kiss.

When Thomas broke away, Alyssa tugged his shirt over his shoulders and scooted to the head of the bed. They both shed the rest of their clothing, taking in each other's body. That experience alone was more erotic to Alyssa than anything she had ever done before. Their lovemaking in the past was usually done somewhat perfunctory after the lights were out. It hadn't been any less special, but it never held this edge of heat.

When Thomas joined her on the bed again, his naked body bared before her, he didn't cover her with his length as she thought he might, but instead lay next to her on his side and took her hand.

"I've never felt this way," he whispered, kissing her fingertips. "At least, not that I can remember."

Alyssa momentarily regretted not telling him about their past but remembered it wasn't a silence she was going to keep forever. Just until after his surgery.

She touched his cheek and smiled. "That's why it's called love," she said and then leaned in to kiss him. She took the opportunity to lay over him, pressing their bodies close, skin to skin. His moan made her smile. "I love how this feels, don't you?"

At his nod, she nibbled at his bottom lip and then moved to his scars. His fingers tugged through her hair as she kissed each marred line of his face, wishing she could take the years away. She kissed her way to his neck, where she sucked gently. When she tasted the salt of tears, she pulled back just as he jack-knifed them into a sitting position.

Thomas didn't bother to hide his emotion. Taking her face between his palms, he sniffed and whispered, "I don't know how anyone could hurt you, Alyssa. I'll never take you for granted the way he did."

Alyssa was touched by his vow. "I know." Their bodies were cradled together at their most intimate point but Thomas turned and laid her against the bed, reversing their positions.

"I want you," Thomas rasped, his tears were gone and replaced by a burning desire she felt in the core of his body.

"I'm all yours. Make love to me," Alyssa urged, needing more.

Thomas looked up at her, a teasing light in his eyes, and gave her a devastating smile. "Don't worry. I intend to do just that."

Alyssa closed her eyes and reveled in the sensation of being in Thomas's strong, unyielding arms as he did just what he promised.

SOMETIME DURING THE night, Thomas rolled over into the warm body next to him and draped an arm around her. His dreams once again consisted of fuzzy faces and flashes of red. It had been two frustrating nights in a row now. He took a deep breath and pushed away the fogginess of sleep and focused on the warm flesh underneath his fingertips. Sighing, his lips brushed Alyssa's neck, and he heard her feminine sigh.

"This is nice," he said, his voice hoarse.

"Mmm."

Propping his head on his hand, he looked down at her in the dim moonlight. So beautiful. With skin that pale, it was amazing she didn't have freckles littering the perfection. But no, it was nothing but pure ivory from head to toe. She rolled over to face him and brought his head down for a lingering kiss.

His palm trailed the length of her arm, down her hip and over the smooth curves of her legs. His own body responded accordingly.

"What are you thinking about?" he asked her, when

she gazed up at him with a distant look in her eye.

She quickly looked away. "I was just thinking about where we're going from here."

He smiled and nipped at her ear. "I have a few places in mind."

Alyssa pushed at his chest and looked at him earnestly. "You might have a wife, Thomas. Have you thought of that? You said you didn't remember feeling this way, but what if you have before?"

His mood turned sour the second he realized her train of thought. He shrugged.

"And you slept with me anyway," Alyssa continued. "If it hadn't been me, would it have been someone else?"

"No." Thomas removed his hands from her and rolled onto his back.

"Why not?"

"Because."

She propped herself up on her elbow, looking at him. "Come on, Thomas. Don't shut me out now. We need to talk about this."

"Not now, Alyssa," he exhaled and rubbed his hands over his face.

"Yes, now. If we don't talk now, we might never. You have a home somewhere out there. People who love you."

"What makes you the expert?" He angled an annoyed look at her and sat up, throwing his legs over the edge of the bed.

Instantly, he felt her cool arms slip around his shoulders from behind. "Please. Talk to me about this."

"What can I say, Alyssa?" he snarled. "I'm a nobody. Quite literally."

"Don't feel sorry for yourself."

"Can we do this tomorrow?" He tried to break out of her grasp, but she held strong.

"No."

"Alyssa..." he warned.

"I mean it. There may be people out there who are

searching for you right this minute."

Anger took over his mood. He stood, forcing her arms away. "If someone is looking for me, they sure are taking their sweet time about it. It's been five years."

"You're a private investigator. Surely you have the resources to look for your family."

"And if I do? What then? I walk up to their house and say, 'Hi, you may not remember me since I'm all mangled now, but I used to be your husband. Wanna screw?'" He turned on the bedside lamp and glared at her. These were the very things he tried to not think about. Hatred was too tame of a word to describe how he thought about his previous life and what he might find if he investigated it.

"What if they thought you were dead? What if they've all moved on? Don't you think if you had a wife or parents or siblings out there, they'd want to know you were alive?" she asked.

He shrugged. "I'm perfectly happy where I am. Or at least I was until you brought this up."

Alyssa stood and walked into his rigid arms. Her cheek pressed against his chest and her deep exhale tickled his skin.

"How could you be happy with such a big piece of your life missing?"

Defeated, he wrapped his arms around her and dropped his chin to rest on top of her head. "Because I have you."

"What if you felt this way before I came into your life?"

It was a good question, one he'd contemplated for a while now. Only one answer came to mind. "If I felt this way about someone else, I would remember."

"You have amnesia."

"I might not remember details, Alyssa, but I would feel it. There's no way this kind of thing can just stop existing. When you love someone, they're always a part of you."

She looked doubtful when she looked up at him. "What if it did stop existing?"

"It didn't, trust me on this."

Again, she pressed her cheek to his chest. "I think we have to find out who you were."

"Why?" he demanded.

"We can't a future with a big elephant in the room. We can't just pretend this didn't happen to you. How can we start a life together if you don't know who you are?"

"I'm Thomas Williams. That's all I need to know."

Alyssa pulled away from him and turned her back. She seemed lost in thought.

"Let's just talk about his tomorrow and get some rest," he said.

She whirled to face him, her eyes pleading. For what, he didn't know. "I need you to know more, Thomas. I need you to...*want* to know more."

He looked at her for a long moment. "Why?"

She bit her bottom lip and looked away. "Because we love each other. Right?" At his nod, she continued. "I'm assuming if everything goes well, marriage might be the next step...and..."

As his eyes roamed over her features, he was at a loss for words. Why was this so important to her? "What is this really about?"

"Don't you want to give me your real name if we get married? Don't you want me to call you by your real name?"

Thomas closed his eyes, uncertain of how to make her understand how he felt about his previous life. "I'm at peace with what happened," he lied. "I don't want to beat a dead horse. I've already said it. I'm Thomas Williams. Whoever I might have been before my accident isn't who I am now. Whatever I might have left behind doesn't matter. I'm at peace."

"Who are you trying to convince, me or yourself?"

He should have known better than to try to sugar

coat the facts. Alyssa's uncanny ability to see right through him unnerved him just as much as it relieved him. With a sigh, he sat down on the edge of the bed and ran a palm down his face.

"Okay, so maybe peaceful isn't the right word. But Alyssa, I can't explain to you how I feel. I'm just here. I admit I used to be really angry with my family never finding me. But then I thought maybe I just don't have a family. That kind of thing happens, you know? Maybe I had just moved to a different city and all my old friends just thought I lost contact with them. It would be really coincidental for that kind of thing to happen, but not unheard of. Think about it."

Alyssa walked to him slowly and knelt in front of him, taking his hand in hers. Her round, innocent eyes held a trepidation Thomas didn't understand. Tears welled as she continued to look at him and her lower lip quivered.

"What if...what if it wasn't anything like that?" she asked. "What if you have a wife who misses you and loves you and is hanging on to nothing but a shred of hope you might walk through her door again? What if she can't move on until she has some sort of closure? Or what if you really do have a mother who missed you day and night since you disappeared? Or a best friend who searched for you until he had no choice but to stop?"

Thomas swallowed. He wasn't ready to admit she might be right, but he couldn't tell her she was wrong. He didn't say anything.

"Please," she said, finally.

Unable to deny her anything, he nodded. "We'll figure it out after my surgery."

Alyssa gave him a brilliant smile and stood, throwing her arms around him. "Thank you," she whispered.

"You might not be thanking me for long." He needed to explain to her how none of this would change anything. He pulled her into his lap and held her, closing his eyes. The feel of her body against his distracted his train of thought.

"What do you mean?"

"It might not be pretty if we find there's someone else involved.

There could be a lot of legalities we would have to work out."

"I'm not worried."

He shrugged. "I am. A divorce, child support if kids are involved. A slew of things could stand in our way."

"I don't think it'll be that complicated," she said, sounding sure of herself. He smiled at her confidence.

"Alyssa," he began and moved her so he could see into her eyes. "You need to know if I do this, nothing's going to change between us. At the end of the day, I'll still be exactly who I am right now. I'll still want you with everything I have. We'll still be together, no matter what. This won't change anything, at least not for you and me."

She smiled. "Of course it won't."

He kissed her then, and the fear of the unknown slipped between them, anchoring them to each other's body. A desperate edge took over their embrace and their lovemaking was no longer about exploration, but rather hanging on to the thin shred of happiness they had found amongst the confusion and pain.

Reaching over, Thomas turned out the light. As his eyes adjusted to the dimness streaming in from the coming dawn, he smiled down at Alyssa. Her body lithe and moving with his underneath him caused him to close his eyes as he sent up a thank you for this special gift.

He smoothed her cheek with his thumb and kissed her thoroughly. "I love you," he said huskily as he pulled away.

She smiled so sweetly up at him, his heart couldn't help but tug at the tenderness of it all.

"I love you, too, Thomas," she whispered as he claimed her.

"So much."

It was the best feeling in the world for Thomas to know she would never hurt him. That alone meant more than the five years of his life before he knew her.

Chapter Ten

THE DAY OF his surgery dawned sunny and hopeful. Birds sang a chorus all around Thomas as he stepped out of his house. He almost laughed, thinking about how he felt like he was in some cheesy musical. With the whistled theme of *The Sound of Music* on his lips and a bounce in his step, he walked to his truck. Pulling out of the driveway, he headed for Alyssa's house.

He glanced down at the brown, legal sized envelope resting next to him on the passenger's seat. This surgery and the contents of that envelope contained the possibility to change his life. He knew, after years of speculation, it was going to be for the better. He couldn't believe he'd waited so long...

Not that he'd admit that to anyone.

When he arrived at Alyssa's house, she bounded out with a wave. His heart surged with love and happiness. He jumped out of his truck and met her across the lawn half way as she launched herself into his arms. Laughing, he spun her around and captured her mouth.

When he set her back on her feet and forced himself to pull away, he looked down at her. Her blue eyes crinkled at the corners and twinkled in the early morning light.

"You're in an awful good mood for someone who's about to go under the knife," she said skeptically.

Thomas shrugged, and kissed her cheek. "I'm just happy to see you."

"I missed you," she said with a smile that lit up her whole face.

"Ditto," he whispered.

He led her to his truck and opened the door for her. She noticed the envelope but just moved it to the side as she stepped in. She didn't ask about it until they were on the road.

He shot her a wink and mumbled cryptically, "The first day of the rest of our lives."

Her eyes grew distant for a moment, but she quickly focused again on his face. "I like the sound of that. Now I'm intrigued." Picking up the envelope, she turned it so that she could open it.

"Hey, wait a minute. I didn't say open it."

She gaped at him with rounded eyes. "You mean you're going to say something like that to me and not let me see what it is?"

"Well," he grinned. "Actually, I'm going to tell you what it is when we get to the hospital."

"I have to wait that long?"

He gave her an apologetic look before turning his eyes back to the road. "Yeah, sorry."

She shrugged. "I can't wait."

The radio kept them company throughout most of the two-hour drive to the hospital. Thomas's surgery was scheduled for eleven. They arrived a comfortable two hours beforehand. After Thomas signed in and they sat down in the waiting room, he took her hand and smiled. Underneath her purse, on the floor was the envelope.

He took a deep breath. It was all he could do not to open it before today, and even now, his instincts were to tear into it like a rabid animal.

"Are you going to tell me what's in it now?"

He kissed the back of Alyssa's hand then bent to pick it up. Hesitating for only a moment, he finally turned to her. "I went to see Jerry last night, after I finished up some stuff, just to remind him of the surgery and catch up with him. We were talking about things, and I brought up our conversation about how you wanted me to figure out who I was."

Alyssa raised her eyebrows, waiting.

"He asked me how I felt about it, and I told him I thought it was time to look into it. Mainly because I wanted to make sure I was free to move forward with you."

He noted the tears in her eyes, but she didn't say anything. "Funny thing was, when I told him that, all he did was turn around and reach into a filing cabinet and hand me this."

He could tell Alyssa hadn't figured it out yet. He placed his palm on her cheek and looked at her earnestly. "Alyssa, this envelope has everything we need inside. Jerry researched me when I was first in the accident. I just kept telling him I didn't want to know anything, but he knew all along who I was. You were right. A real friend would find out anyway."

When the meaning of what he was saying dawned on Alyssa, her eyes rounded, and she moved out of his reach. "You haven't read anything inside yet, have you?" A panicked tone laced her words.

He chuckled. "No. I was, uh..." He hesitated, suddenly unsure.

"I was hoping we could do it together."

She visibly relaxed but kept her eyes trained on the envelope. "When?"

"Well, after my pre-op. It usually takes forever for them to get me back to the OR, so I thought we could do it while we were waiting."

Her eyes riveted to his face. "Thomas, that's not a good idea." Frowning, he studied her. "Why not?"

"It just isn't."

"I don't get you. One minute you're convincing me I need to figure this out and the next, you're freaking out.

What gives?"

"You heard Dr. Laska. No stress before the surgery. You don't know what's going to be in that envelope. It could be upsetting or...."

"Wonderful? I could find out that I don't have a wife or kid anywhere and was a total loner until the accident."

"Don't count on it, Thomas."

"A man can hope, right?"

Alyssa shook her head and looked unsettled. He took her hand again and kissed her fingertips. "Let's do it. As soon as we're in my room, let's open this. A new face and a new life. Together."

She shook her head and frowned. "No, not today."

Frustration ate at Thomas. "Is there something you're not telling me?" She looked at him with wide, innocent eyes, and he couldn't help but feel foolish. "I'm sorry, I shouldn't have said that. I'm just really excited about putting this behind me and knowing who I really am."

"You weren't so excited when I had to beg you to do it."

He grinned, remembering their argument. "Better late than never, huh?"

She gave him a half-hearted grin. "I guess."

"Mr. Williams?" a female voice called from the double doors. "They'll come get you when I'm ready. Bring the envelope," he said and gave her a quick kiss on the cheek.

As he walked back with the nurse, a feeling of peace stole over him and he smiled.

Life was good.

ALYSSA CLUTCHED THE envelope between white, clammy fingers.

Sweat beaded her brow and her breath came in short, shallow puffs. The medicinal smell of the hospital was making her nauseous, or maybe it was just the circumstances she had found herself in so suddenly.

What was she going to do? Thomas looked pretty determined to open the envelope before his surgery; it was imperative she find a way to stop him. Looking at the contents could be devastating to him emotionally and could impede his recovery. Not to mention there would be a lot to talk about once he found out who he really was.

Furthermore, how on earth had a small-town investigator found out Thomas's identity, when all of the highest paid P.I.s she'd hired came up empty?

Bowing her head, she neither saw nor heard anything but her thoughts. Falling in love with Thomas was as unexpected as the realization he was the husband she'd looked for over the years. Funny how the second she made up her mind to move on with Thomas the truth made its miraculous appearance. Her life up until now consisted of an over-zealous best friend and eternal, lonely days looking for a man she could never completely let go.

Now she had a wonderful man. A man, who didn't resemble her husband at all, but shared the same DNA. Thomas was a man she was proud to call her own.

Only now, one piece of paper could take all of that away. Yes, she desperately wanted Thomas to find out the truth, but it had to be after his surgery. She didn't want his recovery to be jeopardized because of impatience. It might selfish, but she wanted their world intact for a little longer. Her first instinct was to burn it. She wasn't ready to take the risk that Thomas would hate her for lying. There wasn't any amount of courage that could prepare her for the look she would see when Thomas found out the truth. The thought of hurting him when her absence already hurt him so much made her throat close up. But crying now wouldn't solve anything. Figuring out a way to keep Thomas uninterested in his past until after his recovery was her top priority now. After that, she would deal with the consequences.

Leaning back in her chair, she held the envelope to her chest and sighed. Fifteen minutes came and went and still no one called for her. There was a desperate edge to her emotions, as if she needed to make every moment between them count now. Thomas was a good man, but forgiving didn't seem to be at the top of his list of qualities. She needed to see him again, touch him. Clenching her eyes shut, she waited. And waited. She waited some more. How long did it take to get him ready for surgery? Start an IV? Put on a hospital gown? Take blood pressure?

The longer she waited the more her nerves scrambled. The envelope felt hot in her sweaty hands.

"Ms. Williams?" she heard a nurse call.

It was a moment before she realized the nurse had called for her. She would have been amused by the mistake if the hospital itself wasn't trying her patience.

Alyssa used the important moments it took to walk through the sterile hallways and double doors to gather her wits. For Thomas's sake, she had to be steady.

The nurse pulled back the curtain and revealed Alyssa's husband lying in a hospital bed, clad in a gown and blue markings all over his face. She squared her shoulders and cleared her throat. It was all she could do to hold it together.

"Thank you," she said to the nurse as she left and closed the curtain behind her. Turning to Thomas, she forced a smile. "Hey, you."

He gave her a lopsided grin and held his hand out to her. When she took it, he reeled her in and pulled her across his lap, capturing her mouth. He felt warm and alive. The jovial mood about him today was due to him having the answers he always wanted so close, she knew.

When he pulled away and grinned at her again, she couldn't help but laugh. She felt the knot in her stomach slowly releasing. "Did you bring it?" he asked, looking around and eyeing her purse. "Hand it here."

"Look, Thomas, we should think about this."

"I haven't done much else." He leaned forward trying to grab it, but she moved out of the way just in time.

"I won't let you do it right now," Alyssa stated firmly. At Thomas's raised eyebrows, she raised one of her own. "You know if what's in here is upsetting, it could make recovery much more difficult."

"I'm willing to take the chance, Alyssa. Hand it over."

She could tell by the careful way he issued his words he was getting angry. If she wasn't careful, she would defeat the reason why she didn't want him to look at it in the first place. Taking a deep, calming breath, she spoke softly. "Will you at least meet me half way? It's really important for us to see what's in that envelope together. I just want to make sure we can deal with it the right way. Can we please wait until after your surgery and you're mostly recovered? It would really make me feel a lot better about this."

Thomas studied her and then nodded slowly. "I've waited this long, I can wait a little longer. Especially if it means that much to you."

Alyssa couldn't help but sag with relief. "Thank you, Thomas. It means the world to me." She flung her body across him in a hug. His chuckle warmed her heart.

"No peeking, all right?"

"I promise," she whispered as she sat next to him on the bed.

She wouldn't touch it with a ten-foot pole.

"That was the only thing I had planned to keep us busy until surgery. Now that it's off the table..." He shrugged and sent her a mischievous grin. "You know, I've got an easy access panel in the back of my little hospital gown here. Wanna take advantage of me?"

Alyssa giggled. "I think I'd develop a sudden case of stage fright since the only thing separating us from prying eyes and ears is a curtain."

"There's a bathroom down the hall."

"You haven't thought much about this at all, have you?"

"Well, I thought we would do some celebrating when we found out who I was," he said, pointedly nodding to her purse. "But I'm up for some recreational sex if you are just to kill some time."

Alyssa shook her head, grinning at the man she loved, so different from the first version. "We'll see."

Crossing his arms, he huffed, reminding her of a little boy who didn't get his way. She smiled and tucked her hair behind her ear.

"Are you scared at all?" she asked as she peered at the markings on his face.

He took a deep breath. "I guess a little when I really think about it. I mean, it can't really look any worse. But knowing the potential is there to look a lot better is what scares me. I don't want to be let down."

Alyssa slid her hand into his strong grasp. "Dr. Laska seems very competent. Whatever happens, Thomas, I'm not going anywhere."

"Thanks. I needed to hear that."

Leaning down, Alyssa pressed her lips to his and then smoothed his hair. "Not only that, but soon enough you'll know who you are. And regardless of how you look, you'll have your family back."

Nodding, he said, "Yeah. If there *is* any family."

"You've got me."

His fingers squeezed her hand. "You're all I need."

Silence fell between them, and Alyssa grew uncomfortable. She felt like a traitor. Thomas clearly loved her, and now she lied by omission. She kept trying to tell herself it was in his best interest for recovery. But the truth was she was scared of losing him... again.

How would he deal with the truth? Lying was still lying. It was going to crush him.

When she tried to look at it from his perspective, she wanted to weep. No way would he forgive her. She deserved everything that came at her because of this.

"Thomas?" she asked quietly, her eyes filling with tears.

"Yeah?"

"I love you."

He grinned. "Don't get all sentimental on me now. This surgery is very routine. I've had others just like it. But...I love you, too." When she didn't say anything but rather continued scrutinize the IV in his arm, he tugged her hand a little. "Hey, I was thinking about something and wanted your opinion."

"Sure."

"I know we've moved pretty quickly, but I've always heard that when you know, you know. I've tried to fight it ever since I met you, but...I know, Alyssa. If you're willing to take a chance with whatever is in that envelope and me looking like this the rest of my life, I'd like to talk about our future when this is all over."

A lump formed in her throat and her voice refused to work. How did she tell them someone had just pressed pause on their future for a little while? Just as she opened her mouth to speak, the curtain was snatched back and a big, burly man walked in with a grin on his face. Alyssa reigned in her emotions before she turned to greet him.

"Gettin' butchered up again today, huh?" The man said with a booming voice.

"Shut up, Jerry," Thomas said with a chuckle. "Hey, you haven't met Alyssa yet. Alyssa, this is Jerry, my boss. Jerry, Alyssa Morgan."

Alyssa turned to greet Thomas's friend, holding her hand out to him. When he didn't immediately take it, she looked up, confused.

"Alyssa," he muttered, his voice accusing. His eyebrows drew tightly together and his eyes narrowed.

Everything clicked into place. Thomas's boss. The man who knew everything. He knew Thomas's identity as well as hers. With a pounding heart, she forced a smile and pleaded with her eyes that Jerry not say anything.

"It's nice to meet you, Jerry. It's really great for you to come by and visit Thomas. The doc says he has to stay calm before the surgery, and I'm sure having a friend here will help."

Alyssa moved off the side of the bed to the chair next to Thomas. She looked at Jerry once more, who was still staring her down. He nodded once in acknowledgment and looked away, his mouth in a tight, grim line.

"That staying calm thing is highly overrated," Thomas said, oblivious to the tension between them.

"No, the docs are smart enough to know what you need," Jerry said and sat down on the far side of him in another chair. "I just wanted to stop by and let you know I'm pulling for you. Try not to overdo it afterwards, either. Make this girl of yours wait on you, hand and foot."

Thomas rolled his head in her direction and winked. "She will."

They joked around a little more and Alyssa was happy to see Thomas had found a friend like Jerry. Their relationship wasn't as territorial as Chris and Jeff's had been, and it seemed much more relaxed. They joked and chatted for about an hour about the surgery, work, and unfinished business. When it wound down, Jerry sighed.

"I guess I better head out. Got a call today from the police station. They want me to assist on a missing child case."

"I should be able to get back in the swing of things after a few weeks. If you get too busy though, let me know. I can do research from home."

Jerry stood and patted him on the shoulder. Thomas held his hand out for him to shake and both gave each other a hearty pump. "Take care, man," Jerry said. Up until now, Alyssa had been largely ignored, but this time he nodded in her direction, cocking his eyebrow slightly. "Enjoy your woman while you can."

Thomas laughed and grabbed her hand, giving it a kiss. "You bet I will."

"Take care you two." Jerry's eyes lingered on her as he walked out the door.

Alyssa relaxed once the fear of discovery eased from her shoulders.

"You okay?" Thomas asked her, a worried frown creasing his brow.

She gave his hand a squeeze and tried to reassure him. "Just getting antsy. I'm ready for this to be over."

"Me, too."

She looked away and studied her shoes. She was so torn up inside and the double meaning behind her words was killing her. "It's about time," Thomas said as a couple of nurses walked in. "Seriously, you guys take forever to get the show on the road. It's almost two hours past my scheduled surgery time! Not only that, but I'm hungry."

The nurses grinned at him and patted his leg. "In a few minutes, you won't know or care what time it is or how hungry you are. You'll be sleeping like a baby."

Thomas winked at Alyssa as a flurry of people flitted about, pulling up chords from his IV and placing them across his stomach, taking his blood pressure and pulse and getting some sort of shot ready.

"Can I walk him to the OR door?" Alyssa asked, suddenly terrified. What if something went wrong in there and Thomas didn't make it? She wasn't sure she could live with herself knowing he died without knowing the truth.

"Sure," the nurse said with a smile reeking of pity. "Ready?" another nurse asked him and held up the shot.

"Just a sec," he said and reached for her. She walked into his arms, leaning over the bedrail and hugged him tightly.

"I love you," she whispered. She didn't care if he was sick of hearing it. She'd never tire of saying it.

"Ditto."

Tears gathered in her eyes again, and she fought them back, trying to make sure the last thing he saw was a smile on her face. When she pulled back, he put a finger under her chin.

"Hey...chin up. I'll see you in a few hours, okay?" At her nod, he kissed her softly.

"Remember...today is the first day of the rest of our lives."

"We didn't open it though."

"Doesn't matter. I'm getting my new face today."

"This might sting a little," the nurse called out and inserted the needle into his IV. Within a few seconds, Thomas's eyes rolled back in his head and a smile lifted the corners of his mouth.

"Ahhh, I love this stuff," he mumbled. His hand kept a firm grip on Alyssa's until the OR doors were in front of them. She tried to pry her fingers away, but he pulled her down to his mouth so she could hear what he was whispering.

"Marry me," he said.

Alyssa laughed, knowing he'd never remember the proposal, but it was sweet nevertheless. When he let go of her hand, he cracked his eyes open and winked. With a chuckle, Thomas disappeared through the door.

Alyssa wound her way back through the identical hallways with a smile. She couldn't wait to see the look on his face when she told him about his impromptu proposal.

Then she frowned. How would she tell him they were already married?

When she reached the waiting room and was looking for a seat away from everyone, her eyes landed on a familiar figure, and she stopped in her tracks. Without warning, Jerry stood up and marched over to her, taking her forearm in a tight, no-nonsense way and led her toward the outside door.

"We need to talk," he growled in her ear.

Panicked, she thought about resisting, but she knew that ultimately Jerry held the trump card. One word to Thomas after his surgery and everything was over. She might as well see if she could bargain with him.

"Jerry, you're hurting me."

"Not nearly as much as I'd like to."

His voice sent shivers down her spine, and she couldn't believe the kind man Thomas often spoke of had just threatened her. Even worse, she believed every word of it.

Finally, when he dragged her far enough away from the entrance to the waiting room, he whirled her around and faced her angrily. "What on earth took you *five years* to find him?"

"I've been looking the whole time for him!"

"I don't believe you! A few articles in a newspaper are barely enough to find someone, especially if he's not in the area," he snarled in her face. "That man has been through an absolute nightmare avoiding his past because it killed him when no one came to look for him."

"I did everything I could, Jerry. You can ask his mother and his business partner…everyone. And if you knew, why didn't you come to me?"

That caused him to hesitate, but after a moment, he forged ahead. "I've watched him banging his head against the wall, isolating himself from civilization, all because he was so angry. It's been a long time, Alyssa. Forgive me if I think all of this seems a little convenient."

She held her hands up in defense. "I can't blame you for thinking that. But I'm here now. And thank you for not telling him before the surgery."

"Yeah, well, I'm not stupid."

Alyssa massaged her temple where a dull ache was beginning. "You know, if you were really hung up on finding him, one call to a P.I. could have found him."

"I hired *three*, all of them came up empty!"

"Any P.I. worth his salt could have found him in less

than a week. He even had fingerprints on file from the accident that matched up with a police file regarding his business."

"So what are you saying?" Alyssa asked, a telltale feeling sinking in her gut. She remembered the equipment robbery just before Chris had disappeared. He and Jeff were fingerprinted to test their prints against the robber's.

"I'm saying your P.I.s weren't worth their salt."

With a sigh, Alyssa sat down on the curb, studying Jerry's shoes as he paced.

"So what's your plan to move forward?" Jerry asked.

"He didn't open the envelope you gave him yet, so after he's well from the surgery, I'm going to let him open it. He deserves to know."

"And what then? You're just going to walk away?"

The sun was high above them, making Alyssa sweat from heat and nerves. Birds played happily in the bushes around the building, but she couldn't bring herself to enjoy their innocence. Her life was crumbling right before her eyes.

"I don't really know, Jerry. I guess I'll let him decide. If he wants me around, I certainly want to stay. He's my husband. But if he wants me to go, then I'll leave him alone."

"You're just going to give up on him?"

"No, but I will respect what he wants. He's been through a lot, and I can't push myself on him if he decides he can't look at me anymore. It's his call. I hope he'll come to see his family though. His mother misses him a lot."

"Does she know yet?"

"No, and I need to call her. I promised her I'd call the second I found out." Alyssa lowered her head in shame. "Seems like I'm lying to everyone lately."

Jerry swung around to face her. "Are you lying to me?"

"No! I love my husband." Standing up, she put her hands on her hips. "I didn't even know he was Chris until a few days ago. I saw a freckle on his back that I knew Chris had and that's when I knew. Before that, I pretty much gave up hope of finding him. Before I figured it out though, I fell in love with him. Not the man I thought he was or could be...but who he really is inside."

Silence thickened the air between them. Jerry cleared his throat. "If you hurt him anymore than you already have..." he trailed off.

"I will, Jerry. You know it's inevitable."

Jerry narrowed his eyes on her. "This time, you better at least be around to pick up the pieces when it's over."

"It's his call," Alyssa said quietly.

"No, he's made the calls for the last five years. You give up on him now, it'll kill him."

"I'll do everything I can. I promise."

"I really hope you're not lying this time."

Alyssa closed her eyes and her shoulders slumped. "You just have to trust me. As soon as he's well enough that the stress won't be too much, I'll tell him. That's all I can say."

She didn't see Jerry's frustration in his eyes but she heard it in his voice. "Well, all I can say is if you don't tell him, I will."

Chapter Eleven

ALYSSA TUCKED THOMAS back in bed for the fourth time that day. "Do you need anything?" she asked him, smiling. Not more than two weeks into his recovery, Thomas shared something else with Chris: They loved to be babied when they didn't feel well.

Half of Thomas's face was bandaged and would remain that way until his next doctor's appointment in four more weeks. Alyssa's heart hurt for the pain he tolerated and the whole front he tried to put up showing he didn't need anything. Smoothing his short hair, careful of his bandages, she leaned down and pressed her lips to his.

"I could use more of those," he murmured.

"Gladly," she grinned and kissed him softly again. When she readied to pull away, his fingers speared through her hair and held her close, deepening their kiss. The movement of kissing her caused him pain and probably wasn't something the doctor would approve of. She pushed weakly at his chest. The man possessed the ability to charm her when she least expected it.

"Thomas," she mumbled against his mouth and pried his hand away. "Let's not risk your healing by doing that."

He studied her, looking hurt. "You don't want to kiss me?"

She gave him a motherly roll of the eyes. "You know it's one of my favorite things to do, but taking care of you doesn't mean I make things worse."

"I'm pretty sure you just made things better.

"You're relentless."

"And you're beautiful."

She squeezed his hand and released it. "Are you hungry? Do you need a pillow fluffing?"

The corners of his mouth lifted carefully as he shook his head. "Pillows are fluffed, and I'm not hungry. And you can stop the mother hen act, it's getting on my nerves."

"Okay, good."

"I think I'll take a nap though. The meds are kicking in." His eyes drooped, and he settled against his pillow with closed eyes. "I love you," Alyssa whispered, looking down at her husband.

Then, she left him to his slumber.

She closed the door softly and leaned against it. Every day her life was teetering on the edge. One slip, one wrong whispered word, and it was over. The agony of it all killed her, and she couldn't wait for the next four weeks to be over. But yet, she dreaded it all in the same breath. The mental anguish of keeping such a big secret from Thomas wasn't anything compared to how she was going to feel when he figured out she kept things from him.

Walking downstairs, she started preparing dinner. She planned to make one of Chris's favorites, lemon pepper chicken. Murphy sat on his haunches, waiting for a morsel of food to be dropped.

Alyssa knew Thomas wouldn't have much of an appetite, unlike Murphy, but she would need to eat, and she wanted to keep a supply of food in the fridge for the times Thomas did get hungry. Just as she had battered the chicken, her cell phone rang. Jeff.

She dismissed the call and continued with dinner.

Her cell phone lit up again.

With a sigh, she washed her hands slowly, hoping her voice mail would pick up the call again. But no such luck.

"What is it, Jeff?" she demanded.

"I know you're angry with me, but..."

"No buts... I can't talk right now."

"I just wanted to see how you're doing. You've got family here who is worried about you. You haven't called lately. Chris's mom is beside herself."

"Why hasn't Kathy called me then?"

"She's been busy."

"Well, if she's so worried, she would have found time to call."

"Maybe, maybe not. She doesn't look well to me."

"Jeff, I think you're using this as an excuse to call me. I told you I needed some time to figure things out."

"Fine. How's Thomas doing?"

"Goodbye, Jeff."

"Alyssa!"

"What?"

He was silent for a moment. "I don't know. I just know that I've got a hole in my heart because I miss you."

With a heavy sigh, she hit the "end" button and placed the phone quietly on the counter. Lowering her head, she studied her nails, trying to figure out what on earth to do about Jeff. Every time they spoke she sensed an indescribable change in him, something akin to desperation.

"Everything all right?" Thomas said behind her.

She yelped, whirling around. Her hand flew to her chest. "I thought you were sleeping."

"I needed some water. I called, but you didn't hear me, so I came down. I heard you talking to Jeff just now. Everything okay?"

Alyssa frowned. "I was just thinking about how he's changed. I think he's desperate. He hasn't done anything to scare me though."

Thomas smiled at her with his eyes. "You'll tell me if that changes, right?"

Talking about Chris's best friend this way bothered her. Over the years, Jeff had demonstrated nothing but kindness toward her. Turning to face the cabinet, she grabbed a glass and poured Thomas some water.

Alyssa tried to smile as she handed it to him. His narrowed eyes told her he sensed something was wrong. He kept an eye on her as he drank the water, making her shift uncomfortably. Finally, the glass lowered, and he gave it back to her.

"So....in a few days I'll be able to do a little more. Do you want to have a picnic at your place or go out somewhere? I can tell you from experience it's not that great having to sit around the house for six weeks."

"I don't think you'll be coherent enough in a few days. And I'm fine. I've got plenty of books and the TV. Not to mention you're keeping me plenty occupied."

The unbandaged part of his face fell, and he looked hurt. "You don't want to go out with me?"

"It's not that," she rushed to assure him while trying not to grin at his little boy act. "It's just that I want to make sure your recovery is quick. You've got a lot riding on it going smoothly."

Stepping forward, Thomas pulled her into his arms and looked into her eyes hopefully. Funny how, with the bandages, she didn't need his facial expressions to see what he felt. "I can already tell you this is the best recovery yet. Mainly because I'm not doing it by myself." He shrugged, this his lips tilted upward. "You're here to keep me company."

"I'm here as long as you'll have me," Alyssa said, her eyes lowering in disgrace.

His finger underneath tilted her chin upward and forced her eyes to meet his. "Forever," he whispered then gave her a full smile. Before she could react, his face turned into a grimace and his hand flew to his cheek. "Ow."

Playfully punching his arm, she giggled. "That's what you get for being out of bed. Get back up there, and let me finish cooking dinner. If you nap between now and then, I might allow you to come down here and watch TV tonight."

With another shake of his head, he walked out of the kitchen, playfully clucking like a chicken as he walked up the stairs.

ANOTHER ROUND OF dreams plagued Thomas during his drug- induced slumber between lunch and dinner. This time he ran in a field full of wild, white roses, pushing at them to keep them away from his face, but they kept snapping back to scratch at his cheek and head. Just ahead of him, a blur of red hair was far enough away that he couldn't reach her. He called to her, but she never turned.

Desperate to see her face, he lunged. The roses bit at him, a strange combination of soft petals and angry thorns as his arms met empty air, and he fell. The closer to the ground he got, he could feel the jagged edge of each thorn tearing his flesh, ripping and pulling.

He cried out, reaching for the blur of red. All to no avail.

He jackknifed into a sitting position, but his vision remained blurry. The gauze on his head annoyed him, and he itched to tear it away. Rubbing his eye with the heel of his hands, his vision cleared, and he saw her standing there, red hair and all, exactly like his dream.

"Alyssa," he whispered. He didn't know if it was the pain meds or what, but he felt the urge to weep at the sight of her. "Come here." Ignoring the horrific pain in his face, he held his arms out to her and urged her forward. She willingly came to him, sitting across his lap, wrapping her arms around his shoulders. Her firm hold on him calmed him.

"What were you dreaming about?" she asked him quietly.

"A big field with roses and thorns cutting my face... Something red is just in front of me, but I can't reach." He wrapped a strand of her silky red hair around his finger. "Red just like your hair."

She studied him but said nothing. Swallowing, he tried to push the image out of his mind, but he couldn't. "I think my subconscious is trying to tell me something, but I don't know what."

She tenderly kissed away the remnants of the dream, moving her hands across his body in a relaxing pattern. It didn't stop one part of his anatomy from having the opposite reaction.

Alyssa laughed.

"Sorry," Thomas said. "But I love that you can do this to me. I didn't think I'd ever feel this way about someone after the accident. I didn't expect to feel so loved and safe with you."

"Safe?" Alyssa asked, looking into his eyes.

"Yeah. Safe. You know, it's like coming home when we're like this."

Alyssa blinked at him slowly, giving him that lazy grin he'd come to love so much. "I think the pain meds are going to your brain."

He chuckled. "Yeah. Must be."

Alyssa moved from his lap and stood. "Here's your medication. It's been six hours. Might explain that bad dream."

Once she mentioned it again, the searing pain returned to the forefront of his mind, and he grimaced. "I hate taking those things."

"Take it anyway. At least it muddles your brain enough that you won't remember much when you come off of them."

"Good point," he said and took the pills from her, swallowing it down with a glass of water. "Thanks."

"Sure. I also brought up some dinner if you're hungry."

"I guess I could eat something." He scooted against the headboard of the bed, nestling himself against the pillows. The contents of the plate looked delicious.

Cooking him dinner, fluffing his pillow... He loved that Alyssa wanted to make a home with him. The domesticity made him want to smile...and he would have if it didn't cause him so much pain. Everything about her was perfect. And the best part? She didn't seem to mind and, in fact, appeared to enjoy it.

"Do you want to go downstairs and watch a movie with me?"

"I don't know how much company I'll be. With the pain pills and a full stomach, I might be out soon."

She smiled sweetly. "I don't care. Just don't snore, okay? That gets annoying."

"No promises."

She tugged his arm and he swung his legs over the bed. When he stood, he hooked his arm around her shoulders and kissed her. Alyssa reached up and threaded their fingers together as they walked downstairs.

Arranging some pillows and a blanket on the couch, they lay down together and watched the movie. The early evening cast deep shadows on the wall, but when Alyssa turned out all the lights, it left only a dim light throughout the house. They curled up together, and Thomas inhaled her familiarity.

He tried to focus on the movie, but spooning as they were, his mind wandered. His attraction to her was insatiable, even in pain after major surgery. Sliding his hands up her arm, he kissed her shoulder.

"Thomas," she warned.

"C'mon. You can do all the work. I won't move a muscle. Well, except maybe one."

She laughed as her hand splayed against his thigh, squeezing. "The doc said no physical activity."

"It won't be if you do all the work. It'll take my mind off the pain," he urged.

Her husky laugh told him he was winning.

"I did say I was at your beck and call, right? I'm supposed to take care of you."

"Oh, I need taking care of."

She turned, movie forgotten, and released every last ounce of the pain in his body.

Later, Thomas awoke to the credits scrolling on the screen, and Alyssa nowhere to be found. He looked around the darkened living room and finally saw her on the patio out back, cell phone to her ear. He really hated that man for calling her so much. If it continued, he would have to see about a restraining order or taking care of it himself. Earlier today, after their conversation, Alyssa had held herself stiff and cool. He didn't like it when Alyssa stressed. He didn't like it, either, when she didn't seem to want to talk to him about the man. Something else he'd have to remedy very soon.

He stood up slowly to avoid a head rush and stretched, then walked to the sliding doors, where she left them cracked open. He didn't want to eavesdrop, but maybe he could glean some useful information. Thomas was good at his job and his determination to make sure everything stayed out of their way before they found out his real identity kept him from feeling guilty.

"I want to know why you stopped looking," she said. "I see. And my money wasn't good enough for you?"

What? Was she paying this guy off now? For what? To leave her alone? Was he blackmailing her somehow?

"But I don't believe that." She sounded frustrated. Her body language was stiff again, and she held herself tightly erect with the phone pressed against her ear. She tried to speak softly, but her frustration raised her voice enough for him to hear clearly.

"Yes, as a matter of fact, I have. It's definitely him, but there's no way I'm telling you anything more, I think I've learned my lesson that you big city people can't be trusted."

Alyssa hung up on the man then, but left Thomas feeling even more confused. Big city people? Jeff certainly wasn't someone he'd consider "big city". Who was on the other end of that conversation?

Before his murky brain registered he needed to move, she turned and saw him leaning in the shadows against the door. First surprise registered and then her anger turned on him.

"What are you doing eavesdropping on my conversations?" she demanded, walking to the sliding door and yanking it open so they could see each other clearly in the moonlight.

Never quick to jump to conclusions in his line of business, he took in everything around him: the steady chirping of the crickets, a few frogs singing a night song. The moon was shining down at them, partially obscured by the corner of the house. And there Alyssa stood, in all her fiery glory with flashing eyes.

"This is my house," he said quietly.

"This may be your house, but I'm staying here to help you. There is a thing called respect. Don't go pulling that macho stuff with me." She stuck her hands on her hips, cocking one to the side.

"So he's blackmailing you?"

Momentarily flustered, it took her a moment to realize he had switched gears. "Who?"

"The big city guy you were talking to."

She studied him through narrowed eyes. "Just how much of my conversation did you hear?"

"Enough to know you're in trouble. I just wish you would talk to me about it. I can help, you know. If you need money or something under the table...I have connections to people who can make your friend disappear. Tie him up with legalities over identity fraud and he'll forget all about you."

"What are you talking about?"

Now Thomas was getting frustrated. He scratched his head through the gauze and wished for the millionth time he could take it off. "Just answer my question, Alyssa. Are you in some kind of trouble?"

Her hesitation told him everything he needed to know. "Why didn't you come to me?"

"No, it's not what you think, okay? You've got to trust me on this."

Thomas hated the nagging feeling he got that he couldn't believe her. "Have it your way." Turning, he navigated through his house in the darkness and climbed the stairs. If she wanted to play hardball, so could he.

Except, she followed him up the stairs. "Thomas that was nothing you need to worry about right now," she said. "When you're healed from your surgery, I'll let you worry about protecting me, but right now I've got to protect you, okay? There's nothing that's putting me in harm's way, I promise you that." She grabbed his arm and turned him around. "No one is blackmailing me. It was just a phone call I had to make about a...friend of mine."

"I see. Does this 'friend' of yours go by the name of Jeff?"

"No, it's someone else."

Thomas shook his head. "Do you realize I know very little about you? I mean, I know the basics, but your previous life before you came here is a mystery."

She shrugged and released his arm. "There's nothing to tell. I lived there, I had a job as a teacher and then I moved here after my husband left me. Simple as that."

"But why did you move before you had a new job? Most people move because they have a new job."

"It was just something I felt like I needed to do."

"Because of your ex?"

"In a way, yes."

Thomas bit his lip and shifted his feet. "I get the feeling that you're hiding something from me. I want to know what it is."

It was then that Alyssa's demeanor changed, and he could tell she was trying to distract him.

"That medicine has you paranoid, Thomas. Get in bed, it's late, and I'm tired. You've been a demanding patient today, and I expect no less tomorrow. I need my rest."

He watched from the edge of the bed where he sat as she undressed and put her night clothes on. Slowly, he did the same. He felt her burrow under the covers behind him. He lay back in bed, careful of his bandages and listened to the silence.

"Will you hold me?" she asked softly, her voice shaky as if she might cry if he said no. If Thomas was anything, he was a sucker for Alyssa, even when he knew something stood between them.

"Come here," he said huskily and raised his arm for her to come into his embrace. Once she settled, his mind wandered over everything he had heard her say, but for the life of him he couldn't make sense of it.

Alyssa sighed softly, and her breathing regulated into a deep, calming rhythm that lulled him into a daze.

Tomorrow, he thought. Tomorrow, he'd make her tell him and everything would be back to the way it had been.

Chapter Twelve

THE OPPORTUNITY TO make Alyssa spill the big secret never arose the next day. Or the next.

One month later, Thomas found Alyssa downstairs cooking breakfast after he woke up. He didn't say anything and ignored the hung-over feeling he continued to have over the secrets he knew she kept. Although it killed him that she wouldn't talk to him, he knew nothing would be gained by forcing her into it. He loved her too much for that.

Walking up behind her, he wrapped his arms around her and nuzzled the tender spot on the side of her neck. He enjoyed the feminine sigh that escaped her lips as she leaned her head back against his shoulder.

"Good morning," she chirped with a fake smile.

He kissed her softly, mourning the loss of her real smile that had been replaced by the impostor on her lips. The last month of recovery had been by far easier than any of the others, having her there to help him eased the burden, but little by little, he noticed she pulled away. He wondered every day if it was about that phone conversation or about Jeff.

Or was it about him?

Thomas didn't like entertaining the possibility, but relationships weren't made of stone. She might not love him as much as he loved her. All of the post-surgery care might have opened her eyes a little. A stab in the heart would be better if he had to endure losing her.

When he was honest with himself, taking care of a man like him probably wasn't what she imagined when she signed on as his girlfriend. For the past month he had been difficult and ornery from the pain medication, not to mention impatient. But not one complaint left her lips. Alyssa just plastered the sham smile on her face and did what he needed her to do.

Today, he was going to change that. He wasn't taking as many pain pills, and he wanted to set things right again. He wanted to make her understand life wouldn't always be like this for them.

"Good morning to you," he said, trying to sound happy. He slipped the pan where she was scrambling eggs from her hand and shooed her away. "This morning I'm cooking you breakfast."

She shrugged and took her glass of orange juice to the table, sitting. "I take it you slept well?"

"Very." He winked at her. "Especially after the activities." She grinned then looked away. "Doesn't every man sleep better after sex?"

"Sure," he conceded. "But it wasn't just sex, Alyssa. We made love." He threw a look over his shoulder and grinned at her pink cheeks. "So, you know my appointment with Dr. Laska is two days from today, and I feel pretty confident the surgery was a success this time."

When she didn't say anything, he looked back at her again.

She was so lost in thought he wasn't even sure she heard him. "Alyssa?"

Her gaze snapped to his, and she shook her head. "I'm sorry.

My mind was on something else."

"Wanna tell me what?"

She shifted in her seat and then eyed the pan with the

eggs. "You're about to burn those."

He looked down at the eggs and realized they were done. He swiftly threw them into a serving bowl and onto the table. Seating himself across from her, he grabbed a piece of bacon and toast she had already made and then spooned eggs onto his plate.

Leaning forward, he touched her hand. "You don't look like you slept well."

"I didn't," she conceded and squeezed his hand before worming it away from his touch.

"My mattress too hard for you? Too soft?"

"No," she said with a shake of her head. "I've just got a lot on my mind. I think I need to go home for a little while, after your next visit with Dr. Laska."

The words punched him in the gut. He dropped his fork with a clang and sat back in his seat, reeling from her announcement.

She registered his surprise. "Not permanently. I just have some things I have to take care of."

"Like what?" he demanded.

"Just some stuff with family. I'm afraid I've been wrapped up in helping you lately that I haven't had time to call them much."

Thomas sat quietly, watching her play with the fork she had yet to pick up, avoiding looking at him. "Is this your way of dumping me? If this isn't what you want, I can handle it."

Her gaze riveted to his. "No. Why would you think that?"

"You've been acting different for weeks, and now you're telling me you're skipping town."

She stood and walked around to him, sitting across his lap. "Thomas, I mean it when I say I love you."

Angry, mostly with himself for chasing after such a distant dream, he deposited her on her feet and stood up. "Do you now?" he challenged her, folding his arms across his chest and leaning a hip against the counter.

"Yes."

He studied her and decided she looked nervous. Upset. Worried. What he wouldn't give to take it all away. "Why have you been acting so weird the last few weeks? This didn't start until that phone conversation on the patio right after my surgery."

"Will you just let it go?" she asked with an edge of hysteria in her voice.

"I'm sorry, but I can't stand to see you like this. Whatever it is has you in panic mode."

"It's nothing I can't handle."

"Apparently you've forgotten I'm a P.I. One phone call is all it would take to figure out who you were on the phone with. I can solve the mystery in less than twenty-four hours."

Her lips pressed together in a tight line and her eyes narrowed. "Oh, sure. Pull out the private investigator card. If you really want to know that bad, then do it. Just go right ahead and invade my privacy."

"I don't want to, but you're about to leave me with no choice. I don't know what to do anymore, and if you're telling me it has nothing to do with me, then I'll do whatever it takes. I feel like I'm losing you."

Alyssa swallowed and tears formed in her eyes. "It's not like that. I love you. You'll never lose me unless you don't want me anymore."

After a moment, he swallowed his pride and held out his hand to her. She took it, and then wrapped her arms around his waist in a crushing hug, one he happily received. With one hand on her head and the other on her waist, he held her close, reveling in the moment. He closed his eyes and took a deep breath.

When she angled her mouth up to his, he kissed her deeply, ignoring the pain in his cheek as he explored.

"Let's go upstairs," she whispered when pulled away and she tugged on his arm.

He looked at her, knowing she still tried to divert his

attention, even now, but resolved the second she left, he'd find out what worried her. Because he loved her, he wouldn't let anything happen to her.

And that, he thought, as she led him upstairs, *is that*.

THE DOORBELL CHIMED at exactly seven and Thomas pulled it open. Jerry stood there holding a bouquet of flowers.

"Aw, man, you shouldn't have," Thomas said, holding his arms out for a hug. Jerry rolled his eyes and punched his shoulder as he walked past.

"Idiot," he muttered.

Thomas chuckled and followed him to the kitchen where Alyssa had watched the exchange. She smiled a little too brightly at Jerry, making Thomas do a double take. Wiping her hands on a dishtowel, she took the flowers from Jerry and thanked him softly. She busied herself putting them in a vase. She couldn't look at him now, not when Jerry knew the truth and might spill it at any moment.

Thomas wanted to have a barbecue tonight and invite Jerry over. Alyssa preferred a quiet night with just the two of them since she realized her days with Thomas were numbered. She couldn't believe how fast the last six weeks had flown by. Every day Thomas grew stronger and less dependent on her.

Every day she wondered why she hadn't let him open the envelope at the hospital. At least then the truth wouldn't be eating at her soul. She wasn't someone who could hide her feelings easily, but Thomas was overly perceptive, and she couldn't blink the wrong way without him noticing.

She felt like a spoiled brat. Here she stood, given precious time with her husband, and she wasted it away with worry. She heard his laugh behind her and smiled. Taking a deep cleansing breath, she vowed she wouldn't let the next two days be ruined over fears. She didn't want to think about it, but did little else. She would simply take each moment as it came.

If Jerry told Thomas the truth tonight, nothing could stop him. Turning with the vase and flowers, she took the gift to the center of the table and arranged them. "Jerry, really, they're beautiful. Thank you."

He gave her a genuine smile. "You're welcome."

"I've got to check the chicken, guys, I'll be right back," Thomas announced and walked out onto the patio to the grill.

"Stop looking like a cornered puppy," Jerry said the second Thomas slid the patio door closed. "I'm not saying anything tonight. You can relax. Enjoy the evening, okay?"

With a nod, Alyssa rolled her shoulders.

"I know you looked for him, Alyssa. I have to say I owe you an apology for thinking the worst at the hospital. I guess I just don't understand why you didn't tell him the second you figured it out."

Alyssa studied him for any sign of dubiousness but quickly decided he was telling the truth. "Because by then things had gone too far, and I didn't know what to do. Now there is the recovery to worry about. It's killing me to keep it from him, and he sees it. He even threatened to investigate me."

Jerry looked over her features and then nodded. "I'll take care of him. But, after he's done recovering, you're on your own. It'll only be a matter of time before he wants to open that envelope."

Alyssa ran a hand through her hair and nodded. "You're right. Thank you, Jerry. It means a lot to me that we're on the same side now."

Jerry nodded once, then disappeared through the sliding doors onto the patio. She could hear the men talking and their occasional laughter. The sounds of home, of family, of friends. Alyssa didn't want to lose it all again.

She knew she couldn't stop the full speed train of destruction, headed straight for her.

DARK AND OMINOUS clouds hovered low in the sky and pelted fat droplets of rain against the hood of the truck as Thomas and Alyssa drove down the interstate to his doctor's appointment. Gross as the weather was that day, Thomas couldn't help the excitement.

The itchy bandages were coming off, and he got to see his new face. Then, as soon as he got home, he could begin to fill in the missing pieces of his life so he and Alyssa could move toward a new life.

He glanced at Alyssa. As usual, she stared straight ahead, her shoulders back and her chin high. Over the last couple of days, she had tried a little too hard to convince him that everything was okay. Out of respect for her, he hadn't used his skills to find out what had haunted her since that phone call. But after today, all bets were off. If she didn't open up to him, he would have to break her trust.

He didn't know where that would leave them.

He couldn't stand to see her so upset, and he wished with every fiber of his being she would talk to him. Thomas wanted to trust their love enough to think that Alyssa just didn't want to burden him with a minor problem, but with her demeanor...her whole being stretched so thin she could barely function didn't leave him with a warm fuzzy in his belly.

Thomas kept a careful eye on the road and squeezed her knee. "A penny for your thoughts?"

Her gaze darted to him and then quickly back to the road. With a shrug she said, "Just thinking about how happy you must be that your recovery is almost over."

It took all of Thomas's might not to roll his eyes. They both knew her mind was a million miles away from his recovery.

"Yeah, I am," he agreed. He moved his hand from her knee and propped his arm against the window, rubbing his forehead. It was exhausting trying to figure her out.

Her hand slid over his, grasping it and bringing it to her lips. "I hope this surgery is everything you've hoped for."

"Me, too." The excitement he felt earlier slowly dissipated, turning into a scorching anger.

"Are you okay?" she asked.

"Yep."

"Thomas..."

The question in her voice did it. He ripped his hands away from her and shot her a glare. Maneuvering through traffic, he turned his hazard lights on and pulled over on the side of road.

"What are you—"

"I can't believe you, Alyssa. Who are you trying to convince more, me or yourself? I haven't bought this fake act of yours for weeks now. That phone call on my patio changed you and you haven't had enough faith in me or our relationship to tell me what's going on." He took a deep breath and forced his gaze away from her. The rain came down hard, but his mind was anywhere but on the weather.

"I told you it was nothing, why won't you believe me?"

"If it's nothing, then you're okay with me finding out who you were on the phone with that night?"

He saw her hesitation, but her chin lifted as she met his gaze. "If it's that important to you, go ahead."

"It wouldn't be so important if everything about you hadn't changed. Or is it just me? Can you honestly tell me that you haven't changed? Or have you decided against being with me? You say you love me, but your actions say otherwise. And believe me, Alyssa, whatever is really going on can't be any worse than what I've imagined."

Alyssa lowered her head and studied her nails. "I guess I never considered it from your perspective."

He rolled his eyes. "I'll say."

"I'm sorry, Thomas." She didn't elaborate any further which made him even angrier.

"Are you going to open the envelope tonight when we get home?" she finally asked.

Releasing a pent up breath, he pressed his lips to-gether. "Yes. Maybe then I'll have at least *some* of the answers I've been waiting for."

"Don't be like this."

"Me?" he argued, gritting his teeth. "You're the one who's completely shut me out. If you can't trust me enough to tell me what's going on, what kind of future do we have?"

Alyssa's eyes rounded. "I don't know."

Too angry to speak, Thomas fell silent and studied the steady rhythm of the windshield wipers, desperate to calm down.

"Can you just trust me for a little bit longer?" Alyssa asked, unbuckling her seat belt and moving closer to him. "I promise I'll answer all your questions...soon. I don't want to talk about this today, okay? Today is a happy day."

The gentle persuasion of her palm against his band-aged cheek forced him to look at her against his better judgment. Her eyes shone with pain and confusion, and he ached to take that away from her. His protective instincts took over, and he considered it ironic he wanted to save her, even if it was from herself. If only she would talk to him and ease the burden, maybe he could make things better.

"I love you, Thomas," she whispered, barely audible over the pounding rain.

"Are you sure about that?" His voice remained deadpan, but his eyes searched hers for a hint of hesitancy.

"I've never been more positive of anything."

Her answer pleased him, but he still felt like he was in quick sand. "Love doesn't keep secrets."

She closed her eyes and shook her head slightly. "I know. All I can ask of you is to just give me a little more time, and I'll tell you everything. Can you trust *me* enough to let that happen?"

He took another deep breath. What else could he do? If he wanted to keep her, this was obviously important. Did he trust her, as she asked him? Should he demand she trust him? A catch twenty-two, indeed.

"What choice do I have? I can't make you talk to me." Moving away from her, he put the car in gear and eased back into traffic. They didn't have to wait long at the doctor's office since they were one of the first patients of the day. Thomas said a silent thanks for that because he still stewed inside. He needed something to take his mind off Alyssa.

In the room, Alyssa waited quietly in the corner. The only telltale sign she was even alive was the quick tempo of her bouncing foot. A quick glance confirmed her nerves were as shot as his.

Dr. Laska entered just as Thomas settled, clad in his usual white coat, stethoscope around his neck.

"Good morning, Mr. Williams," he said with a huge smile. Thomas couldn't help but smile back and extend his hand.

Some of his excitement returned as they went over the last six weeks. This was his moment. Everything was riding on his new face.

If Alyssa wasn't being truthful and living with his scars was proving to be too much for her, this surgery could change all of that. Even though his gut told him something different, his rational side couldn't help but think his scars might play some role in her change.

"Well," Dr. Laska announced and placed his chart

aside. "Let's get these bandages off. I'm sure you're ready."

Thomas nodded and turned his back to Alyssa. He heard the rustling movement of her standing. "Why don't you step out, Alyssa. I'd like to see this for myself before you do."

"Don't worry," Dr. Laska added. "He just wants a chance to beat me up if I didn't do it right this time. The nurse can show you where the coffee is."

Behind him, Alyssa said nothing. Thomas heard the door open and click softly shut.

"Things not going so well?" Dr. Laska asked as he found the end of the gauze.

"Just a rough patch...I hope." Thomas's mood wouldn't allow him to discuss his love life with his surgeon. His foot rapped against the floor impatiently.

"Relax," Dr. Laska urged.

Finally, Thomas felt the first layer of gauze lifting. And then another. And another. The first wisps of air touched his skin. He sighed in relief, and his foot started to bounce again in anticipation. "I have to say, I'm a wonderful surgeon," Dr. Laska pointed out. "But I outdid myself this time." He stepped back and admired his handiwork. "Wow," he said as he motioned to the mirror above the sink. "Take a look at the new Thomas."

Thomas stood up. He walked to the mirror, his eyes trained downward on a droplet of water in the sink. Slowly his eyes rose, almost of their own accord, until they shifted to see his new face for the first time.

A rush of air escaped his lungs and tears flooded his eyes. His fingertips traced the corner of his eye, once down-turned and jagged, now smooth and pink. Only a small line remained. He opened his eyes wide, testing for pain, but found none. His cheeks still glared an angry red from the surgery, but he could tell once they healed up more, it would be a drastic improvement. He looked...*almost* normal.

A smile spread on his face and threw his head back and laughed. Turning to Dr. Laska, he extended his hand. "Thank you, doc. This is more than I hoped for. It looks great!"

Dr. Laska pumped his hand several times then nodded toward the door. "Wanna call her in? I'm sure she's on pins and needles." Thomas's mood darkened a little. Would his new face be enough for her? He nodded, but turned back to the mirror to examine his face as the doctor let Alyssa inside. "He's a new man," he heard him say.

"Yeah, Alyssa, I am. You're not going to believe this." Smiling, Thomas turned around and looked at her.

He saw a cup of coffee fall from her hands, splattering against the tile floor. Her hands flew to her mouth as she gasped and tears welled in her eyes.

"Chris!"

Chapter Thirteen

ALYSSA DIDN'T KNOW why she was so shocked at Thomas's pensive mood on the drive home, not to mention the fact he hadn't uttered a single word to her. Instead, he drove with his eyes straight ahead, knuckles white and his beautiful new face scrunched in thought.

When they pulled up at his house, Thomas didn't even bother to open the car door for her, something he always did. He simply walked inside and slammed the door, not once looking back.

This was it, she had lost him, and he didn't even know why yet. Had saying his name out loud triggered a memory? What would happen now?

Alyssa chose to give Thomas the space he needed and walked around the neighborhood in the waning light until she found herself standing in front of her own home. Her dark house loomed before her, but her mind stayed with Thomas. She hated how she had left things, but wasn't it better it had happened now rather than later?

More time would only leave a bitter taste in Thomas's mouth once he found out the truth.

Entering her house, she walked numbly through the dark, climbing the stairs to her room. She removed her earrings and watch, putting them on the dresser in the crystal dish Chris had given her for their third anniversary. Trailing a finger across the edge, she closed her eyes momentarily, remembering the happiness she used to feel.

Why did it suddenly seem so far away now?

For the last five years, everything was so unsettled. And for the last few weeks, everything had finally fallen into place again, even before she had known the truth. Finally ready to move on, one word—one name—caused it to go up in smoke. The feeling was gone again.

"You want to tell me who Chris really is?"

Thomas's voice caused her to gasp. She fumbled in the dark for the lamp on her dresser and the light threw the room into dim shadows. Whirling, she saw him sitting in the chair in the corner of the room in a deceptively casual pose. One ankle rested on his knee and his chin was propped in the L his fingers created. Only his eyes gave his anger away.

He looked dangerous.

Alyssa walked around the dresser, her heart in her throat, and sat on the foot of the bed so she didn't have to face him. For a long while, neither of them moved as she tried to figure out how exactly to tell him what he wanted to know.

Lost in thought, it wasn't until his boots came into her line of vision that she snapped her gaze up to his. He intimidated her, standing there with his hands on his hips and a determined glint in his eyes. He cocked an eyebrow, reminding her he waited for an answer.

Alyssa stood in order to deflect his intimidation. His face looked so much better since the surgery. While some scars still littered his skin, which was normal, most of the imperfections in his eyelid and cheek were completely absent. His mouth now quirked in an angry line and his jaw pulsed.

"Who is Chris?" This time his voice rose and punctuated his words in staccato. He had reached his limit, and she knew it.

Alyssa looked away and bit her lip. She studied a speck in the carpet and frowned, tears forming in her eyes. The speck blurred and, as she closed her eyes, the tears fell down her cheeks.

"You," she whispered, her voice shaky. She sniffed.

"What?" he asked, leaning forward.

She looked up at him, watery eyes meeting steel ones. Taking a deep breath, she repeated, "*You* are Chris."

For a moment, Alyssa saw the shock in his eyes as he digested the information and everything fell into place. Then, as if a steel door rolled down his face, his features became blank.

"You have to understand..." she started and placed a hand on his arm.

He snatched away from her touch and pointed an accusing finger at her, his eyes cold and dead. "How long have you known?" Alyssa put some distance between them. She walked around the bed and stood against the wall next to the closet. She swallowed. This wasn't how she had envisioned this conversation going. When she didn't immediately answer, he marched in front of her again, taking her arm in his strong grasp. "How long?"

She couldn't do anything to stop the out of control, downward spiral her life had taken in the last twelve hours. "I wasn't sure until the night we made love. You have a heart-shaped freckle on your back."

He released her, holding his hands up in the air as if he were being arrested. Then he swung them down with a slap against his thighs. "I should have known," he hissed between clenched teeth.

"I'm sorry, Chris."

He whirled around on her, his eyes spitting fire. "My name is Thomas."

Alyssa pushed away from the wall, her anger returning in spades. Just because he was different now didn't mean she loved him any less. "No, your name is Chris Morgan. You're my husband."

He glared at her but said nothing.

"And I love you." Those words she issued softly when she thought she witnessed a crack in his demeanor. But his narrowed eyes told her it was misplaced.

"If you loved me, we wouldn't be having this conversation *now*. And my name is *Thomas*."

"Your name is Chris Morgan," she insisted. "And you have every right to be mad at me. I understand that. I won't listen to your sob story about how no one cares. For the last five years, I've searched for you and put my life on hold. I've wondered about you, cried over you. And now that I've found you again, there's no way in the world I'm going to let you push me away because you've told yourself lies about me."

"You don't have a choice in the matter."

Alyssa narrowed her eyes in his direction. "Your truth isn't necessarily *the* truth, Chris. I was there. I *know*."

"Oh yeah?" he snarled. "What do you know, Alyssa?"

A lump formed in her throat. "I know you love me. I know your smile. The sounds you make when you wake up in the morning. I know how you make love to me and how you shuffle your feet when you're nervous."

She noted how he shifted his feet subconsciously then.

"I know you sing in the shower. You write little messages in the fog on the mirror for me to find when I shower after you." Alyssa smiled. "You never let us go to bed angry. You leave shoes in the middle of the floor and half the time I'm convinced you did it to drive me crazy. You hate coconut and your worst fear is being alone."

He took a few steps toward her, lowering his face so his nose touched hers. "Self-fulfilling prophesy, huh?" he snarled.

Alyssa shook her head. "Only if you want it to be."

He shook his head. "I don't know what I want."

Taking his hands, she looked up at him in earnest.

"*Today* can be the first day of the rest of our lives if you'll just let it be."

"Let it be? You lied to me!" he shouted.

"I didn't know at first, and by the time I did, I was afraid of this. Of you being so angry and not believing that I still love you. I loved you before I even knew you were Chris."

"How am I supposed to believe that? I waited five years for you. I've finally moved on, and you want me to go back."

"I want you to come home where you belong."

"I am home." His face turned red and his hands shook.

His anger was justified. She just prayed she could find the right words to make him understand how much she loved him. "Your mother misses you. She's been through so much waiting for you and never giving up. You have a life to rebuild, Chris."

"My name is Thomas," he yelled. He turned and grabbed a vase from her dresser and hurled it against the opposite wall, shattering it into a million pieces of broken memories. His breath pumped in and out of his body, and his fisted hand clenched and released. Slowly, he looked at it, raising it so that he held it away from his body.

He turned shocked eyes on her.

"Oh, God," he said, closing his eyes on the whispered prayer. They opened to look at her. "It was me? I'm the one who left you."

Alyssa swallowed and nodded slowly. "You didn't mean it."

"You don't know that. *I* don't know that."

"Yes, I do," Alyssa said. Of all the things they could rehash, that was the last thing she'd have thought of. In all the time she'd been with him, not once did she think history might repeat itself.

With slumped shoulders, Thomas sat on the bed and shook his head. He stared straight ahead into his thoughts.

She sat next to him, not daring to touch him, but yearning to do nothing more. She wanted to seize the opportunity to pull him into her arms and make his world right.

"This whole time I've wanted to remember my past, and now I'm not sure I ever want to remember. Any man who could accuse you of cheating and then leave without finding out the truth..." He choked back his tears and blinked. "I couldn't live with myself."

Alyssa couldn't stop from touching him then. It surprised her this weighed so heavily on him, even more than her lying about his identity. Entwining their fingers together, she squeezed. "We had something special. When you left me, it was out of anger and frustration. I did something that led you to believe I cheated. It was my fault."

When he looked at her, it stole her breath. Agony lanced through his features, and his brows creased in a worried frown. "So you're just letting me off the hook? I was just angry and frustrated and it's all your fault? I played no part in it?"

"I've never believed for a second you leaving was permanent. We loved each other." She moved so she stood in his line of vision. "We still love each other."

Thomas shook his head and pressed his lips together. "*Did* you cheat on me?"

"You saw me with Jeff, goofing off when we arrived at Natalie's apartment at the same time. You worked a lot, and I spent more and more time at her place in the evenings so I wouldn't be alone. You noticed how much I wasn't home and followed me one night. He put his arm around me and kissed me on the forehead." She shrugged. "You assumed the worst." Frustrated, Alyssa sighed.

"Why was he kissing you and putting his arm around you?"

"He always told me I'm like his little sister. We goofed off all the time like that before you left. We were all close friends."

He looked at her long and hard. Alyssa's gaze didn't waiver. "And now?"

"I told you I never cheated on you."

Thomas stood and kept his back to her. "I know, Alyssa. But it's not just that. The lack of memories." He shook his head. "Everything. The man you describe is nothing like me."

Alyssa couldn't agree more. "You're opposites in fact."

He looked over his shoulder but turned back to the darkened window of her bedroom. "How is it possible to love me if I'm so different?"

Alyssa shrugged. "I don't know, to be honest. But I'm not questioning it. I think we've been pretty lucky to find each other again. For awhile there, I lost hope I'd ever find you."

He threw another look over his shoulder and propped his hands on his hips.

"I love you." She caught herself when she almost called him Chris. When she really thought about it, she didn't think of him as Chris. "Thomas," she added.

He turned slowly, running a hand down his defeated features. "I can't do this right now."

Panic surged in her chest, and she stepped toward him. "Please, don't shut me out."

"You just told me who I am, a fact I'm accepting blindly because somewhere underneath all your lies, I still trust you to tell me the truth about something this big."

"Then we can build on that," she said frantically, tugging on his arm. She hated how pathetic she sounded, but she couldn't help but feel like the rug was slipping out from underneath her again.

"I've got a lot to digest right now," he explained. He gestured between each of them. "Our relationship is something I really have to think about."

Hurt and angry, she lowered her head and allowed the tears to fall. Losing him wasn't something she could endure again, despite the certainty of it all.

She felt his finger lifting her chin, and her gaze sought his.

"Thank you for..." He swallowed and pulsed his jaw, his eyes bright. "Thank you for finding me."

All Alyssa could register was his words held a finality she couldn't accept. "Don't leave," she begged, hating herself for being so weak.

"I have to." He turned and walked away.

She watched him until she couldn't see him any longer, and then took off after him. "Fine. Just leave the same way you did five years ago. Just walk away from me," she sobbed. "I can't believe you're doing this to me again."

Sobs wracked her body, and she held onto the banister to keep her balance. When Thomas reached the front door, he turned saddened eyes on hers. For a moment, she thought he might come back to her. His hesitancy hurt her more than anything. She had never hesitated to love him or search for him.

He hurt her all over again.

"I'm not doing this *to* you, Alyssa," he said in a quiet voice. "I'm doing this *for* you."

With that, he walked out the door, closing it softly behind him.

Alyssa collapsed on the bottom step and doubled over with tears. When he left her five years ago, she only *thought* it hurt. The pain in her heart at that moment didn't even compare.

THOMAS COULDN'T GET home fast enough. When he threw his front door open, he crossed the living room with shaking hands and tore open the envelope Jerry had given him before his surgery. All the stat sheets, credit reports and police reports for a missing Chris Morgan were there. Wife: Alyssa Morgan. Fingerprints from one of Chris's former jobs and a police report of stolen machinery at a business he owned were lined together on a sheet of paper next to his own, one that Jerry had taken the day he hired him. The nail in the coffin was final, indeed.

Sitting on his couch, he tossed the papers to the side and buried his face in his hands. He'd go over everything in detail later. But he wasn't surprised. Not in the least. And in fact, when he was honest with himself, something deep inside of him always knew. Now the question wasn't who he was, but what did he plan on doing about it?

How could he trust Alyssa after keeping something like this from him? Could he believe her when she said she feared he wouldn't be receptive? He certainly hadn't embraced her and asked to remarry her. He also hadn't given her an answer one way or another on where their relationship went from here.

Then he thought about all she must have gone through to find him. He might have had a good reason to be angry with his family before he met Alyssa, but now his reasons were shot. Alyssa had searched for him. Three separate newspaper articles, one dated five years ago, another two and a half years ago, and the last one dated just eight months ago proved she had actively looked for him. Did he just blindly accept who she was and go back to the life he had before? Did he disregard the man he had become after the accident?

With a sigh, he stood and grabbed his keys. He couldn't escape the fact that Jerry had known about him from day one and neglected to tell him. His boss had also met Alyssa at the hospital. Boy, would he have loved to be a fly on the wall for that conversation.

Knocking on Jerry's front door a half-hour later, Thomas didn't wait for an invitation to come inside. Jerry just shot him an uncertain glance and closed the door behind him.

"The doc did a good job on the surgery," Jerry praised, motioning toward his face.

"You can cut the crap, Jerry. She told me." Keeping his temper under control wasn't his strong suit, but he was trying. The more time that passed, the angrier he grew.

Jerry's brows lifted. "Told you what?"

He turned on him. "Who I am."

Jerry shrugged. "That was all in the envelope I gave you."

"The envelope you know I never opened."

Jerry shrugged again and walked around him. "You've carried a chip on your shoulder since the day I found you, Thomas. Any man in his right mind would have wanted to find his family. But you just held a grudge."

"And that makes it okay to keep who Alyssa was a secret from me?"

He held up his hands in defense. "Hey, you're the one who insisted all these years. When she showed up, I figured it was best for you to learn your own lesson."

Thomas bit his tongue to keep a nasty retort inside. "You're supposed to be my friend."

"And you're supposed to have a brain in your head. Just because you're missing a few memories doesn't mean it's completely jacked up. You still have your common sense."

"She's my wife, Jerry." The word felt funny rolling off his tongue, and he frowned. "You should have at least told me to be careful."

"If you ask me, falling in love with the same woman twice is a blessing. If I had told you who she was, you would've written her off without a second glance. I think I did you a favor."

With clenched teeth, Thomas said, "You didn't do either of us favor. I left her, Jerry."

That put Jerry on the alert, and he took a step toward him. "What?" he demanded.

"Before this happened. I left her. I thought she cheated on me, and I left her. Karma is coming back to haunt me."

"Why?"

"Some stupid argument, or so she says. I just can't help but think she's wasted five years on finding me when she should be moving on with someone who wouldn't do that to her. It makes me question who I really am."

Jerry took another step forward. "Just take a deep breath. You've been given a lot of information in a short time." Thomas did as he suggested and breathed.

Jerry studied him, then finally laid a brotherly hand on his shoulder. "For the record, I tried to give you that envelope many times, but every time I brought it up you told me you didn't want to think about it."

Thomas nodded and folded his arms across his chest. "What else was I supposed to do?"

Jerry smiled and gave him a firm pat. "A girl like Alyssa shouldn't get away again. And I'm sure you'll resolve everything after you've had some time to cool down."

Thomas wished he could smile and agree with him, but he was far from knowing what he should do. He was a private investigator. He busted others for lying. How had he not seen this coming?

He never thought he would have the wool pulled over *his* eyes. "Thanks," Thomas sighed and walked to the door. "I think I'm going to need a little more time before I go back to work. I've apparently got a family who misses me."

"I understand. Take your time. I'll be here when you're ready to get back to it."

"You know what I just don't get, though?"

"What's that?"

"Why it took her so long. She claims she looked for

me for five years, the papers did articles on the fact I was missing. When my prints were on file, and I worked for you, why didn't someone find me sooner? It's not like I was hiding."

Jerry nodded. "Ask your old buddy, Jeff. He has all the answers you need."

Thomas tried not to get his back up, but it felt near impossible not to. "I'm a big boy, Jerry. Just tell me and maybe I can fit the pieces together."

Jerry shook his head before the words were out. "You've got enough going on without me butting into your business. It's not my place anymore. Now that you know who you are, the rest is up to you. You should just focus on yourself and Alyssa right now."

With a nod and a sigh, Thomas left.

What did he do with himself now? He longed to see Alyssa and make sense of everything all jumbled up in his mind. He had a million questions about his past and the kind of man he was.

He couldn't go to Alyssa. His emotions were too unstable and the last thing he wanted to do is hurt her again.

As he looked up at the night sky, ebony satin with pinholes for stars, he reminded himself that he had survived losing his identity, had survived a mangled face. He had survived a life of complete uncertainty for five years now.

Surely he could survive finding out his past.

Couldn't he?

ALYSSA SAT ON her back porch, sipping hot tea and wiping her tears. The unknown had always scared her, and right now terror clawed at her. All the years she had searched for Chris and suddenly he appeared. Only right now, he was about as far away as he could get.

All because she hadn't believed he could handle the

truth.

She ran her fingers through her hair, sighing. What did she do now? Go to him? Leave town? Wait?

First, she promised Kathy a phone call.

Blinking away her tears, she dialed Kathy's number. It was late, but she knew she wouldn't be in bed.

"Hello?"

"Hi, Kathy, it's Alyssa."

"Hi, sweetheart. Are you okay? You sound upset."

"Yeah, I'll be fine. I think it's time I called you."

"About Chris?"

"Yeah." Alyssa leaned her head back and closed her eyes. It would be a feat to convince her to not get in the car and come straight to Thomas's house.

"I'm assuming by your tears, you've found out that man isn't him?"

She could hear the desperation in Kathy's voice, and it almost undid her. "Chris is still alive, Kathy...I found him."

There was stunned silence followed by loud sobs. "Put my baby on the phone!"

Alyssa hesitated. "Kathy, I need you to listen to me." After a few moments, the sobs grew quiet and Alyssa spoke again. "Chris was injured...he has amnesia."

"What?" The soft, broken question told her she didn't comprehend what that meant.

"Chris has no memory of you or me. His face was badly injured and the portion of his brain that holds his memories was damaged. He's had surgery to correct the scars and he looks really good, but he's not the man who left us. He's pretty much the opposite."

"What do you mean? When can I see him?"

"I just told him today who he was. He's having a hard time dealing with it. We're both going to have to give him some time to come to terms. You have to re-member, he's been living his life for five years without us. I'm not sure when he'll decide to see us again. It's best for

Chris right now to let him have some space."

"Of course," Kathy said with another sob. "I always knew he was out there."

Alyssa lowered her head. "Me, too."

And yet, he was still out there. Without his family. Without his friends.

Without her.

Chapter Fourteen

THOMAS SAT UP all night, piecing together the puzzle in his fragmented mind. Everything about Alyssa made sense now, from her determination in the beginning to her hesitation at the end. Sleep finally claimed him only a couple of hours before he heard knocking on his front door. Knowing it was Alyssa, he debated for a few moments before heading downstairs. A box about knee-high sat at her feet but her eyes remained carefully averted. He didn't want to admit the feeling of relief that washed over him at the sight of her. Even knowing she'd kept the truth from him didn't stop him from loving her or stop him from wanting to gather her in his arms and hold on tight.

Clenching his fists at his side, he waited for her to speak first. Silently, she bent down and hoisted the box in her arms and strode past him, side-stepping Murphy, who lay near the door- way. She went straight to the kitchen and placed the box on his dining table. He watched as she kept her eyes anywhere but on him. She took a deep breath. "I'm leaving."

The momentary stop of his heart and then the subsequent kick of it restarting caught his breath. Slowly, Alyssa's eyes traveled upward and met his. The torment he saw there almost made him forget about her lies.

Somewhere inside of him, he knew it hurt her almost as much as it had him for her to keep the truth hidden. There was another part of him, the desperate part that feared keeping her in his life was an act of selfishness because of the loneliness he endured. If only he could remember the circumstances of their fight. Why he had felt it was necessary to leave her? Had he seen more than she was willing to admit? It might make the answer more black and white for him.

Even thinking that, he realized there would never be an excuse large enough to justify even *thinking* about leaving her, not if their love was as unique as it was now.

How did either of them know?

"Why?" he croaked, taking a step forward.

Regardless of her deception, he didn't want her to leave. He didn't want to spend the next five years wondering if he'd made another mistake.

The open window in the kitchen allowed a slight breeze through and the smell of roses surrounded him. He inhaled deeply, hoping it wouldn't be the last time he ever smelled her delicate beauty.

"I contacted your mother and told her you were still alive. I didn't think it was right to keep her in the dark any longer. I need to go home and do damage control and make sure she doesn't come here and force herself on you."

Thomas nodded slowly. It was his turn to look at the floor. The urge to hold her grew and that worried him.

"And you said you needed space. If I stay here, I can't give you that." Her voice wobbled, and he looked up to see tears pooling in the depths of her eyes. Her blink sent them racing down her cheeks. Her chin quivered, but he saw how much it cost her to let go in front of him.

"Alyssa—"

She held up a hand and continued to speak, a note of desperation in her voice. "Every ounce of me demands I stay here and help you remember, make you love me again. But there's a part of me that's terrified the end will still be the same no matter what I do. I can't deal with that now, Thomas. It hurts too much. I just found you again...I didn't think I'd ever have to let you go."

He took another step forward, and she retreated equally.

"I thought you might want these," she said, motioning to the box. "It's all of our pictures, start to finish. It might help you remember. You don't have to look at them, but it just seemed like you might be interested in seeing your previous life. But I understand if you don't want to. Just keep them, they're yours."

"I never said this was over, Alyssa."

"But you never said it wasn't."

"I just don't know right now." He looked out the window then shook his head, confused.

"When you do, you know how to find me." She hesitated, then added quietly, "I'll never stop waiting, Thomas."

She turned to walk away, covering her mouth as a sob tore from her throat. His arm reached out and grabbed her, his eyes imploring.

"Don't do this to me," he begged, his defenses breaking down and a lump forming in his throat.

Her gaze settled on his mouth, then her eyelids lowered. "I'm not doing this to you, Thomas. I'm doing this for you."

Wrenching away from him, she put one foot in front of the other until she was gone.

Thomas felt the emptiness creep into his soul the minute she left. He stood in the kitchen, wondering what to do next. Should he go after her? Should he trust his heart right now?

Thomas sensed within himself more confusion than he fathomed. His feet refused to move. Yet his heart was with her, wherever she was headed.

Looking down at the box, he decided to look at its

contents and give them both some time. He ran his fingers through his short hair and sighed. No one had warned him life could be so difficult. He wanted to curse Alyssa for pulling him out of his comfort bubble. Before she had come into his life, he had been perfectly content *not* knowing anything. Now, he seemed like a greedy kid at Christmas. He wanted all the answers, all the knowledge he'd once possessed.

Even as he thought that, he knew he was just telling himself he was content before. How angry and lonely his life appeared without Alyssa in it. Everything changed knowing she was gone. The world was less vibrant, the sun a little dimmer. The sparkle he put in her eyes was replaced by sorrow over the turn their relationship had taken. If only he could go back and change everything.

If only...

Peeling away the tape on the box, he looked inside. Several photo albums rested inside as well as an envelope with his name on it. He opened it first, knowing whatever Alyssa wanted to say to him wasn't going to be easy to read, no matter how much he loved her.

Thomas,

Writing this isn't easy. Knowing that I'll be leaving to-morrow hurts me, but I know it's for the best. I have to go back home and let your friends and family know you're still alive. I spoke with your mother tonight and nothing can compare to the relief she felt at the news her son wasn't gone.

We never gave up hope, Thomas. Not me, not your mother, not Jeff.

Jeff was your best friend and helped me search for five years until I came to this town. He decided to go back home to continue his life without us. You owned a landscaping business together up until you disappeared. Jeff kept the business after you left. It was struggling once, but now it is thriving, and I hope you can one day come home to it. I see at your home that you still love to landscape. Perhaps your subconscious remem-

bers more than you do, I don't really know.

I can't believe that Chris just stopped existing. But please know, no matter what, I love you both.

She went on to give him dates and details of their life together. Thomas was still floored over the fact that he could be friends with someone like Jeff. Shaking his head, he read on. Near the end, Alyssa concluded...

There's nothing I want more than for our life to just pick up where we left off, but I realize now that it isn't possible. I'll never stop waiting or wanting you, Thomas. You said once that when you love someone, they are always a part of you. I know that's true for me. You'll always have my heart and my soul.

I can only hope one day you can say the same.

I love you, Thomas. I love you for the man you once were, the man you became and the man I know you still are.

THOMAS PUT THE letter down, fighting back tears. He shouldn't feel this empty over something he'd done to himself. It shouldn't hurt. But it did, more than any surgery or physical pain he'd endured. This was quite possibly the worst pain he had ever imagined.

Taking out the first album, he discovered it was their wedding pictures. Tears puddled in his eyes, but he wouldn't let them fall. He did still have a choice in all of this.

Rubbing his eyes to clear his vision, he viewed the first picture. He inhaled sharply as he viewed his wife in her wedding dress.

It was the same.

The dress was the same dress he saw in his dreams. Her red hair flowed around her shoulders, much longer than it was now. The veil on her head was full and traditional, and the tiara the same one he dreamed of.

What did that mean?

Holding his breath, Thomas realized it meant only one thing.

Those dreams were memories. At least, parts of memories.

For the first time since realizing Alyssa's betrayal, he felt hope. Was the impossible possible? Could he defy the odds and get his memories back, despite what his doctors told him? Could he remember who Chris really was? Could he be the man that Alyssa wanted him to be?

He wanted more than anything for this whole nightmare to end.

Flipping through the albums, he was amazed. He and Alyssa were so happy once. Every picture radiated that love.

How could he believe Alyssa wouldn't be faithful to him?

Then he came to the pictures with Jeff. Both of them looked so young. Alyssa mentioned they had started their business right out of college. He and Jeff had their arms looped around each other's shoulders and smiled ear to ear. Behind them, a grand opening banner hung across the front door of *Rock Solid Landscapes*. Even though he was a private investigator now, he could see how he had once loved to plow his fingers through the dirt. He still did.

But the familiarity of it all was lost to him now. Five years was a long time to be away from something. Even longer since his memories were lost.

For hours he sat there, looking through page after page of pictures, over and over again. He willed his mind to recognize something, anything. But only the dress and Alyssa's face felt familiar. But he would build on that. He had to.

Soon, the sun sank below the horizon, and he lowered the pictures. He leaned back, tired and overwhelmed with the life he used to live, so different from the one he made for himself since the accident. In the dark, he couldn't help but think how lucky he was Alyssa had even felt compelled to stick around. Everything about him was different. Could it be true that she really had been drawn to him, regardless of who he was? It was the only logical conclusion.

Of course, he didn't discount that a part of her, whether conscious or not, recognized him. It did put a whole new perspective on things, though.

Standing, he walked into the kitchen and grabbed a bottled water. Thomas went upstairs, confident his life was about to turn around. If this happened at any other time, he would have been resistant to the truth. But here, all alone in the darkness of this house, a place he could no longer call home, he realized one thing.

Home was anywhere Alyssa wanted them to be.

ALYSSA WASN'T SURE how she made it home. On the long, tearful drive back to her hometown she had waged a war over turning around and continuing on. She couldn't help but feel like she had given up. She was the one leaving him now. What message did that send Thomas?

But she kept telling herself he'd asked for space. She had seen the finality of his goodbye in his eyes. Thomas may not remember being Chris, but she knew what that look meant. His words may have said he wasn't sure what he wanted, but she knew in his heart he couldn't look at her the same knowing how much she had lied to him.

She was her own worst enemy. But being in a no-win situation from the beginning, she didn't know what else to do. If she had told him right away, he wouldn't have been receptive to her. Since she waited, she lost his trust. What was the right thing to do?

Leaving was all she could come up with. He said he wanted to think things through and giving him time was the answer she kept coming back to.

She drove straight to Chris's mom's house. When she pulled up in the driveway, Kathy was out the door before

Alyssa had turned off the engine.

"Where is he?" Kathy demanded through the window.

Alyssa closed her eyes for a moment, hoping against hope she could convince Kathy to give him some space, too.

Opening the door, she tried to smile but failed. "He didn't come with me."

Kathy's shoulders fell and without a word, she turned and walked inside. Alyssa followed her, at a loss for words. She couldn't imagine the torture that the other woman had gone through knowing Chris was alive but not in her arms yet.

"I'm sorry, he just isn't ready," she muttered, watching her fall onto the couch. Then, she realized Jeff hadn't lied. The woman looked ten years older since the last time Alyssa had seen her only a few months ago. "Kathy? Are you okay?"

Her head jerked up and her eyes glared. "No. I'm not okay. I've waited five years to see my son again, and now you're telling me I can't. Do you *think* I'm okay?"

"No, it's just that...you look like you've lost a lot of weight."

"Worry will do that to you."

Alyssa frowned at Kathy's demeanor. She was always so kind and supportive. Her change in attitude concerned her as well. "Is that all it is? Are you sick?"

"No, Alyssa. I haven't been able to eat or sleep because I just *felt* like this was it. We found him."

"We did." She finally smiled.

"No, we found a man who looks like him. Everything else is different, no?"

"You'll still love him the same. Thomas...Chris is still an amazing man."

"But he doesn't remember us. How are we going to keep going when he doesn't remember anything?"

Alyssa wondered the same thing. By the time she had

learned the truth, it no longer mattered as long as they were together.

"Kathy, you'll find a way. He's just as scared as we are."

Alyssa watched as Kathy bowed her head and sobbed into her hands. Walking over to her, she sat down and put her arms around her, but as soon as her touch registered, Kathy pulled away and held her hands up.

"Please, I think I need to be alone."

Alyssa let out a breath and closed her eyes momentarily. Why, when she needed someone did everyone else seem to want to be alone?

Standing, she gave Kathy one last glance and left the house without another word. Her feet carried her to her car, and she left, knowing she couldn't go home to the place she and Chris had lived together, slept in, made love...

There was only one place where she could go and have open arms waiting for her. She drove there, blinded by thoughts and memories of her and Chris together in happier times.

Knocking on the door of the familiar home, Alyssa allowed the tears to fall freely, surprised she even had any left. She'd always heard what didn't kill you made you stronger, but she was pretty certain the ache in her chest would be the end of her.

The door opened and for a moment, she registered the surprise on Jeff's face just before she fell into his open arms.

Words weren't necessary. His arms folded around her and he held her close, easing a little of her burden with his friendship.

"I'm so glad you're home," she sobbed. "I didn't know where else to go."

Chapter Fifteen

JEFF SMOOTHED ALYSSA'S hair and lent her his strength. Sagging against him, she clung as she cried, terrified her life would never be the same.

Carefully, Jeff ushered her to his couch, sitting down and putting his arm around her shoulders. "What did he do to you?"

Swiping her eyes, she looked up. "Thomas is Chris, Jeff. Chris is alive."

He didn't react immediately. He kept his face free of emotion. "Then why are you crying? The last time you cried like this was when he disappeared." Jeff touched her chin and tilted it up, forcing her to look at him.

Shooing his hands away, she frowned. "I left him to give him the space he needed. He felt betrayed I didn't tell him who he was the minute I found out."

"I suspected it was him, but I hoped I was wrong."

"Why? I thought you would be happy. I was...until I realized he never wants to see me again."

Jeff didn't say anything but rather studied her with an intensity she didn't understand. Suddenly, he rose and walked away from her, running his fingers through his hair.

"You know, this is all for the best. You were better off without him anyway. I warned him before he left he wasn't good enough, and it looks like I was right."

His words caused the hairs on Alyssa's neck stood on end, and she felt paralyzed. Her silence must have alerted him.

"Well, it's true," he protested as he swung around to face her. "He took everything from you, marrying you so young. You deserved better than him."

"But..." she hesitated, frowning. "He was your best friend. How could you say that?"

Jeff carried on like she hadn't spoken. "I warned him this would happen. That you were going to throw your entire life away marrying him."

"But I didn't."

"Didn't you?" Jeff countered, arching an eyebrow pointedly.

"You wasted all your time while he was in school, waiting on him hand and foot. You never even took time for yourself until he graduated. Then he disappeared and you spent five years looking for him. Now you're no closer to your happily ever after than you were before you met him."

"Where is all of this coming from?" Standing, too, she kept her gaze trained on him, wondering how he could turn on the man who had shared so much of his life.

"How could you not see it was him from the beginning? You supposedly knew him better than anyone, yet I took one look and knew. You found out the hard way."

"You knew?" Understanding dawned. "That's why you left, wasn't it? You were hoping I'd follow you."

He nodded and bit his lower lip. "You should have known," he accused.

"It was an honest mistake. Very little about him is the same. He doesn't kiss the same. His voice is similar and the laugh is the same, but he speaks differently. He doesn't touch me the same. Thomas's personality is different, he's more muscular, and he dresses different-ly..." She looked to Jeff once more and saw the resolution in his eyes.

"All of which can be explained away by amnesia and a little weight lifting. You know?"

Alyssa felt panic setting in. "How did you know?" she whispered, her mind running over and over again the possibilities.

She kept coming back to that moment in the hotel when Jeff had tried to get her to leave. She remembered how Jeff tried to convince her it wasn't Chris, and they needed to move on.

Then she thought of the night in the pool hall and how she'd forced herself to remain seated and not get her hopes up that the man who had Chris's profile was actually him. Had the scars blinded her from the truth? Or had Jeff kept her distracted enough not to notice?

Jeff's jaw pulsed, and he ran his fingers through his thick hair.

"The scars make it obvious."

"No, you tell me the truth!"

"It was when you told me he had a motorcycle accident that I knew for sure."

"But Chris didn't have access to a motorcycle. There was no record of him renting one, no one we knew owned one and there wasn't one found. He would have had to borrow a motorcycle or stolen one and even that would have been registered. The owner would have eventually reported it missing. They have VIN numbers for those very reasons."

Jeff hesitated. "What if it was someone who knew him, though? Someone who just bought a motorcycle?"

"No one I know had one around that time." Alyssa bit her bottom lip and frowned, trying to remember that far back. She looked up at Jeff for an explanation. "What if..." Her words died away when she saw the sweat beaded on Jeff's brow and the tight, drawn line of his pressed lips.

"Alyssa," he whispered, his eyes bright.

"No." Her heart raced, and she felt sick.

"I thought it was stolen," he said, stepping toward her.

"Did you not notice the coincidence, Jeff?" Her voice edged on hysteria, the shrillness of it harsh even to her own ears.

"Can I explain?"

Tears blurred her vision. She wasn't sure if she wanted to hear this or not. More lies from a man she thought she knew. "I think you better start from the beginning."

Jeff reached her and urged her toward the couch. They sat down and Alyssa stared, unable to comprehend how Jeff managed such a betrayal when he claimed to love her.

"There were some robberies in my neighborhood a few weeks before my bike was stolen. I didn't think anything about the connection between the two until later. I mean, once Chris went missing, my motorcycle was the last thing I was concerned about. I had just bought it a few days before and hadn't registered it or anything. About a week after Chris's disappearance, I got a call from a policeman from a town about an hour away from here. He said he'd traced the VIN back to the guy I just bought the bike from and he'd given him my information. My bike was found, totaled on the side of the road in his town. I chalked it up to whoever stole it dumping it there and ate the loss." By this point, Jeff's eyes shimmered and his voice wobbled.

Alyssa simply sat there, too numb to know what she should think or feel.

"It never even crossed my mind that there was a connection until you said Thomas told you he was in an accident. The second we got off the phone, I went back through my records and found the date. Sure enough it was stolen the same night Chris went missing."

"And you expect me to just believe that it never dawned on you that Chris might have taken it?" Alyssa demanded.

"I don't expect you to believe anything, Alyssa. But I promise you on everything I own that it's the truth."

Alyssa just shook her head. "I think I need to go."

"Please, Alyssa. At least I'm coming clean."

She stood and walked to the door with Jeff at her heels. "I need to leave," she said quietly.

"You have to believe me," he pleaded with her, his hands on her shoulders, urging her to turn.

"How can I believe anything you say?" Finally she faced him, and she knew she couldn't hold it in any longer. "Did you really expect me to be so forgiving when something like this was right under our noses to begin with?"

"I don't expect anything from you."

"Did you really not put this together before now? Or did you turn a blind eye because you thought this was your way to get in my good graces?" Alyssa yelled at him.

"Whoa," Jeff said. "I guess I deserve that, but I can tell you, when Chris went missing, the last thing on my mind was stealing you away from him. But I've loved you for as long as I can remember. I can't help but feel we'd be good together."

Alyssa felt so confused and angry she couldn't help herself. "We're not good together. We're horrible together. You only remind me of Chris and what I'll never have again. And now? Now I can never look at you the same, wondering if you've led me on a wild and deliberate goose chase!" Defeated, Alyssa wilted, covering her face and sobbing so violently she could barely breathe.

"*He's* the one that led you on a goose chase. For five years and then the second he walks back into your life, there you are again, taking whatever crap he's feeding you," Jeff said. "We fought at work that day because I told him you'd never be happy with him, and it was best to leave town and not look back. I told him I could appreciate you better. The night before he disappeared I warned him he'd never be enough for you. And he wasn't."

Stunned into silence, Alyssa tried to fit the pieces of the puzzle together. But nothing made sense. She turned and examined him, realizing she knew nothing about the man before her.

"What exactly did you tell him? I want to know everything."

He ran another frustrated hand through his hair. "I'm telling you. You deserved more than that shack of a house you lived in. You deserved more than your husband accusing you of cheating with his best friend. You deserved more than what he gave you. You deserved *me*. Because I loved you enough to want to make you happy."

She took a step forward so they were nose to nose. "Chris gave me everything. Our house was our *home*. We loved it. He worked long hours to give us a better life. I never complained, and I understood why he did it. I appreciated him working so hard for us and our future. I loved him, Jeff. I still love him."

His eyebrows furrowed in anger, and he stabbed a finger in her direction. "That's always been the problem, huh? You've always loved *him*."

Suddenly, everything snapped together like a magnet hovering over a paper clip. "This was never about him, was it?" she asked quietly.

Jeff looked away and didn't answer.

"This was always about your feelings for me. Unreturned feelings, I might add." Her anger rose, and her vision blurred. "You just wanted me and the business all to yourself. You knew he watched us at Natalie's apartment, didn't you? You wanted him to think we were sleeping together. And *you* made him feel like the business failing was his fault."

Again, Jeff remained silent.

"Answer me!" she shouted, tears forming in her eyes.

"Alyssa, just calm down."

"Don't you patronize me. I want an answer. Did you

know Chris was watching that night? What did you tell him? And what did you say to make him feel like a failure?"

"Chris told me many times he was upset that you weren't home in the evenings. He started wondering if something was going on. So, I told him the truth. That if he really loved you he'd be home with you, making sure you weren't bored enough to go elsewhere. He told me he was going to watch you, so I made sure he saw something."

"You're a jealous fool."

He shook his head and looked away, propping his hands on his hips. "I love you, Alyssa. I've told you before. We could be happy. But if you're determined to love that loser, what else can I do?

"Even if Chris doesn't want me, I could never be with you."

Jeff rolled his eyes. "It's not about that anymore. I just..." She was surprised to see tears in his eyes again when he turned to face her. "I just want you to be happy. I don't care who you're with as long as I can see you smile. You never smile anymore."

"My reason to smile disappeared because of you," she whispered.

Like a deflated balloon, his shoulders sagged, and he walked over to his couch again and sat down. Elbows on his knees, he ran his fingers through his hair. A slow, forceful exhale left his lips.

"I'm sorry," he finally said, his tone void of emotion.

"I think you should tell Chris that, not me."

He shook his head, his eyes rising to a point on the wall, lost in thought. "It's just that for the last five years we've been together almost every day. I came to depend on you. I guess I thought that over time, things would just happen between us."

"But it didn't, Jeff. And it won't. And the bottom line stays the same. You guilted Chris into leaving. *You're* responsible for what happened to him."

He nodded, as if he finally understood.

One last thing came to her mind as Alyssa looked at Jeff sitting there. The night Thomas overheard her on the phone, the night that started the end of their new beginning.

"Did you pay off the private investigator in New York?"

Jeff's bloodshot eyes focused on her. "What?"

"I spoke with him. He said someone asked him to quit looking for Chris and paid a lot of money. Did you have a part in that?"

She registered his frustration as he swallowed, obviously thinking of a way to hide the truth. But it was much too late. She saw it in his eyes, in the careful way he looked at her.

"Yes or no?"

He looked away. Anger boiling in her blood, she grabbed an empty can of soda and hurled it across the room. It hit the wall with a shallow clang, much too silent for the rage she felt.

"Answer me," Alyssa demanded. "Did you call off the private investigator?"

Finally, he stood again, licking his lips. "Just tell me how to make this right again. Tell me how to get things back the way they were, when we were friends, and you were happy."

Tears brimmed and flowed over her cheeks, but Alyssa barely registered them. She spoke through gritted teeth. "Give Thomas his life back. Sign over the business to him, since it was his in the first place. And give him a heartfelt apology for all the damage you've done. Make sure you tell him I never touched you. And after that…"

He looked at her, waiting.

"Stay as far away from me and Thomas as you possibly can. I *never* want to see you again."

Jeff's jaw ticked, and his face betrayed his anger.

Alyssa felt nothing inside as she sent Jeff a final glare and left his apartment. The extent of Jeff's damage didn't fully settle on her until she reached her home. Sitting in her car, she debated going inside. Nothing but memories were inside the small home, and Chris still filled every corner. Would that ever change? Would her life ever stop feeling empty?

Jeff's manipulations left yet another hole inside of her. She once called him a friend, even considered him family. To know that the entire time she had spent looking for Chris, Jeff was thwarting her efforts hurt her more than she thought it could.

What a pathetic mess her life had turned into.

THOMAS CRAWLED INTO bed and hiked the covers up to his chin. Yet another day spent looking at pictures, hoping against hope just one would trigger a memory. But there was nothing but an empty space where his memories should be.

Six days had passed since he'd last seen Alyssa. His arms ached to hold her, and his heart longed to see her smile. She was so beautiful when she smiled at him. Knowing he caused that smile made him feel good.

He couldn't go back to her as only half of the man she loved. It didn't matter she said she loved them both; she deserved more. He would keep searching the abyss of his mind until something came out of it. He knew it had to still be there. His entire being couldn't just disappear.

The doorbell rang downstairs just as he drifted off, and he cursed his heart for jumping at the thought it might be Alyssa. His mind, however, reminded him of the "For Rent" sign in her front yard telling him she was long gone.

He took the stairs two at a time and hurtled the door open, just in case his mind was wrong.

"Chris." Jeff nodded once and pushed his way inside

without invitation.

"It's Thomas," Thomas said through gritted teeth.

"Thomas."

"What can I do for you? It's late." He wanted to keep this civil, but something in the look on Jeff's face told him it could get ugly quick.

Jeff finally stopped just inside his living room and turned to face him. "I'm in love with your wife," he announced without preamble.

Thomas couldn't help but chuckle. He wasn't even sure what was funnier, the fact he had a wife or that Jeff thought he wasn't privy to the breaking news. "Do you want a medal for your honesty? Why are you here?"

Jeff shuffled his feet and cleared his throat. "I'm also someone you used to call your best friend."

Thomas rolled his eyes. "You've missed the boat, my *friend*, I already know all of this."

"I know, I just...I came here to let you know I'm sorry. I've done some really rotten things to you, and you don't even know it."

"Like what?" Thomas didn't like the sound of this and braced himself.

He sat down and listened as Jeff told him all the ways he had thwarted Alyssa in hopes of her falling in love with him, how he kept her from finding him until she insisted on coming to the town he knew he lived in.

"And Alyssa and I never had an affair," he said finally. "She would never cheat on you."

When he fell silent, Thomas gathered his thoughts.

"What did I do to make you hate me so much?" he finally asked.

Jeff looked him square in the eye and replied, "She chose you."

Confused, Thomas tried to figure it all out. "Was this always between us? Did she give you any indication that she could feel the same way?"

"No. I just thought with time I'd be able to convince

her she didn't need you."

"And now?" He knew it was important to hear it out loud, just as much for Jeff as himself.

"Now I realize I made a mistake. The only time I've ever seen her happy was when she was with you. But it really burns me that the saddest I've ever seen her is when she's with you. I just hope you don't screw it up."

Thomas looked at him but didn't say anything.

"Anyway, I came here to give you this." Jeff leaned over and handed Thomas a thick envelope.

"I'm responsible for you losing your identity...Thomas. I'd like to give it back to you."

Thomas opened it and saw legal documents inside. Frowning, he asked, "What's this?"

"Our...your business is yours again. You were always better at it than me anyway."

"Alyssa said it was doing really well now."

Jeff nodded.

"I can't take this. I don't remember how to do landscaping. I'm a private investigator now. It's all I know."

"Alyssa suggested that you might want it back. She also suggested that I leave town. It's the only thing left I can do that's right."

Thomas thought of his life and how answers were finally becoming clearer. Leaving Alyssa must have felt like the right thing to do in order to give her a better life. Now, he understood that leaving her had cost her her own life.

He looked at Jeff and understood all he had given up for someone he used to call a friend and woman he loved.

"I can't do that to you, Jeff. If we used to be friends, then we still are. Alyssa has taught me a lot, and one of those things is forgiveness. I can't make you start over."

Jeff frowned.

"Your identity is Rock Solid Landscaping. It's not mine. Moving away won't give me the last five years back. It won't even make Alyssa and me stronger. The only thing it accomplishes is the very thing I'm trying to avoid, and that's running from my problems. As far as I'm concerned, if you stay away from Alyssa and give us time to get back on our feet, everything else will happen with time."

Jeff seemed to mull this over for a while. "Alyssa won't be happy about me staying."

Thomas nodded. "I'll deal with Alyssa."

They walked together to his front door, and Thomas extended his hand. "I appreciate your honesty," he said, meaning every word as Jeff shook his hand. If Jeff was a bad person, he wouldn't have come, confessing his sins. "These belong to you." He handed over the envelope with the legal documents for the business.

Jeff looked at them for a moment, and then accepted them. "Thanks, man."

With a nod of understanding between them, Thomas watched as Jeff left. Closing the door, he smiled. It would take some time to get over the things Jeff had admitted to doing, but he had faith his life was finally coming together.

Chapter Sixteen

THE NEXT MORNING, Thomas showered and shaved and donned his best clothing. He knew what had to be done now.

For days he had hoped for some sort of glimmer from his past, something that made him believe he still had a life to go back to. Something he could give back to Alyssa. In all honesty, he wasn't sure *what* he had looked for, but he knew he'd recognize it when it came.

Last night, he recognized it.

The dream began as they all did...a massive field of wild flowers and white roses, only this time there were white chairs decorated with ribbons waving in the breeze. An archway at the front held twisted white roses. He watched as the occasional petal flew free and drifted along the horizon.

Thomas turned and saw people standing all around him. Their muffled voices meant nothing. A few slapped him on the back and congratulated him. But why? He closed his eyes, trying to remember. What did all of this mean?

When he opened them again, he stood under the archway with a man in a suit. Jeff stood to his left and to his right was a woman he didn't recognize wearing a champagne colored evening gown. He assumed it was

Alyssa's friend, Natalie.

Everyone was sitting down now, looking behind them. The wind lifted his hair and he touched it. It was longer than he could ever remember wearing it. He touched his face and felt the smooth skin of his cheek, the stubble of a five o'clock shadow.

He looked again to the woman at his right in the dress. She smiled sweetly at him and nodded with her head toward the crowd.

"Look," she mouthed.

His gaze traveled back to the crowd, and settled on the end of the aisle. It was her. The woman with fiery red hair. He couldn't see her face for the veil and a sinking feeling settled in his gut.

He watched as she walked toward him, like an angel in white. He couldn't move, nor could he couldn't breathe. Finally, she was in front of him, her face still halfway obscured. He reached up to remove the veil. He wanted to see her.

Slowly, as the veil lifted from her face, she smiled. The pent-up breath he held released, and he smiled back.

Alyssa.

He knew it. Something in his gut kept telling him that.

"Are you nervous?" she whispered, her voice satiny smooth in his ear. A thumb traced circles against his skin.

"How could I be nervous when I'm about to have everything I've ever wanted?" He felt his cheeks rise in a full smile, the movement feeling awkward. "I love you."

"I love you, too. Let's do this."

The minister led them through their vows as they placed wedding bands on each other's fingers. He realized he remembered that moment in time, even in his dream. Seeing Alyssa that way, looking a little younger than he knew her to be, amazed him.

She beamed up at him with excitement. The promise of their new life together dancing in her eyes humbled him beyond words. He thought of the vows he had just spoken to her. Words were so inadequate next to their love, but they would have to do.

Jerry was right. Falling in love with her twice in a lifetime was a precious gift. One he wasn't going to throw away.

He grabbed the envelope with the addresses in it. Murphy followed him into the cab of his truck. He'd made boarding arrangements for him until he returned, hopefully with Alyssa.

Two hours later, he pulled into his mother's driveway. It felt odd, knowing he wasn't going to remember the woman who gave birth to him. But he owed it to her to come and see her first. Seeing Alyssa would take some time, and he hoped he didn't have to leave her again anytime soon.

A woman and a dog stood on the porch of the house as he got out of the car. The afternoon sun shone on her face, and he could see the tears on her cheeks. They were weathered and slightly wrinkled, but she was an attractive woman for her age.

His heart went out to her. How hard it must have been all these years, wondering if he had died. If her worries were any worse than his wondering, he was surprised he wasn't visiting her in a padded cell.

"Are you Kathy Morgan?" he asked, just to be sure. At his voice, the dog lurched down the porch steps and came to his side, tail wagging. He patted the dog's head, but riveted his attention back to the woman.

She didn't come down the stairs and at first he thought she was unable to. But as he approached her, finally standing within arms length of her, he saw her shoulders shaking and heard her quiet sobs. Her nod confirmed his question.

All these years he thought no one cared for him, but seeing her now with puffy eyes and a tissue clenched in her fist, he knew he'd had it all wrong. His mother and his wife loved him more than anything...and still loved him.

He searched her features for any trace of familiarity, but his brain once again came up blank. Instinctively, though, he knew she was his mother. It was a weird feeling to have no physical memory of her, and even stranger to feel the invisible pull toward her.

"Mama?" he asked, surprised to hear his voice wobbled. He rushed up the stairs when she held out her arms and felt the comforting feeling of being there. She smoothed what little hair he had and kissed his temple. He imagined this was what it felt like when he was a little boy. A safe haven.

Love.

"I don't have any memories of you," he said with a note of apology in his voice.

"It doesn't matter, baby. We'll make new memories." Her sweet, tearful smile made his chest ache.

She turned and motioned with her hand and they walked inside. He followed, unsure of how things would go. So far so good, but he couldn't shake the uneasiness.

"I have some pictures here I thought you might want to look at," she said. "Do you want some lemonade? It used to be your favorite this time of year."

"Uh, sure." Thomas hoped she wouldn't force the memories on him. For the first time, he was ready to learn about who he used to be, he wanted to remember, but that didn't mean he still had to be that person. A lot of changes had taken place during the five years he'd been gone.

"Your father would be so happy that you're home," she said as she poured the glass of lemonade.

He caught her use of past tense. "He died?"

She nodded solemnly. "Right after you and Alyssa married. Heart attack."

Thomas felt a measure of relief that he hadn't died while he was missing. How horrible would it be to know his own father had passed without resolution? "Who takes care of you now?" he asked her as he opened the first page of baby book his mother had made for him.

"I take care of myself, Chris. Alyssa and Jeff check in on me a lot, too."

He straightened. "Speaking of Jeff..."

Kathy held a hand up with her lips pressed together tightly. "He came by here earlier this morning and told me everything."

"And?"

"And that boy isn't welcomed in my home anymore. He detoured every avenue we had to find you. This could have been resolved years ago if he hadn't stopped us."

"Alyssa asked him to move away."

At the news, she looked up. "Is he going to?"

"No. I asked him to stay. Nothing changes regardless of where he lives."

Kathy nodded, her gaze settled on something beyond him. "I suppose not, but it's going to be hard for me to forgive him."

Thomas took her hand and squeezed. "But you will, I have faith. We've all got a lot of forgiving to do."

Tears welled in Kathy's eyes, and she squeezed him back. "I love you, son," she said.

Thomas swallowed down the lump in his throat. "I know," he whispered with a smile.

With a shaky breath, she released his hand and turned to the albums. Then, she began to tell him the true story about a boy named Chris.

WITH THE CHANGING of the seasons came unpredictable weather and Alyssa was no stranger to it. Her own life was as unpredictable as the storms: one moment she basked in the warmth and joy of the sun and the next tears fell as the rain did against the windowpane. She sat on the couch, looking out the window behind it, wondering what Thomas was doing.

The first thing she did when she came back into town was check with the school about her old job. They had already filled her position but were still looking for a fifth grade teacher. School was scheduled to start in a matter of weeks, but still Alyssa couldn't pull herself together long enough to appreciate the fact she even had a job. All she wanted was Thomas.

Thankfully, Jeff kept his distance. Time hadn't dulled the pain of his betrayal. Just thinking hurt, about the years she had spent wondering about Chris, never giving up.

Going crazy.

Yet, Jeff had known all along and kept her from finding him. She knew she would never be able to look at him the same way again.

With a sigh, Alyssa pulled the blanket from the back of the couch. How had things turned into such a mess?

The gray light turned into night, and Alyssa turned her TV on, sick of her own thoughts. She didn't want to think anymore. She didn't want to *want.*

The TV illuminated the cozy living room as shadows danced and played around her. She tried to focus on the show, but her mind kept straying. Outside, the rain picked up and a boom of thunder caused her to jump.

Just when she felt sleepy and thought about heading to bed, a knock pounded against her front door. Her first thought when she heard the urgent knocking was that someone ran off the road and was hurt. She jumped up from the couch, throwing the cover back and rushed to the front door. She swung the door back on its hinges, prepared to help.

She stopped in her tracks, taking in the beautiful sight before her.

Thomas, dripping wet and with the most serious look on his face, stood in front of her. His elbow rested against her doorframe, and he towered over her short stature.

For a long moment, they simply stared at each other.

He licked his lips and swiped at the rain on his face.

His eyes were red and his cheeks flushed. He straightened himself into his full height and took a deep breath. With a soft voice, he said, "I, *Chris*, take you Alyssa, to be my wife."

Her heart stopped beating and lodged in her throat. The rush of tears made her whimper.

"Even when we're poor or wealthy. Even when we're sick or well. Even when times are bad or good. Our life together is the most important thing to me, and I promise to always put you above my job, my friends, my family and most importantly, myself." He stopped and swallowed, his eyes shining.

If the rain wasn't still running down his face, she could have confirmed he was crying. She, too, couldn't stop the flow. She didn't know what all of this meant, but she was unable to think straight.

"I promise to love you every day of my life and be the best husband I can be. I promise to hold you if you're weak, comfort you if you're sad, help you if you're sick, and make sure you never doubt the love I feel for you. Today, Alyssa..." He took a step forward and grasped her hand, his grip strong and sure. "Let today be the first day of the rest of our lives."

Standing there, Alyssa tried to sort through the myriad of feelings going through her. Happiness, sadness, love, caution, hope...that was only a few. But love won out.

Squeezing his hand in return, she recited, "I, Alyssa, take you *Thomas*, to be husband."

When she smiled at him, she saw his face crumple. He didn't wait for her to finish, he stepped inside her house, dripping wet, and took her face in his hands. As he crushed their lips together, Alyssa couldn't help the surge of joy and relief flowing through her. She fell against him, loving the feel of his arms holding her again, just as she had imagined for the last month.

"Do you remember?" she asked against his lips, unwilling to separate from him.

He shook his head. "This whole time, I kept dreaming of a woman with red hair in a white dress, even before I met you. I just thought it was a dream until I saw our wedding pictures. Then last night, I finished the whole dream. And it was a memory. I asked Mama about it to be sure."

She pulled back to look at him. "You've been to see Kathy?"

He confirmed her question with a nod.

"I bet she was so excited."

"She is a great woman. I'm happy to know I have a family now."

"Are you?" she questioned without confidence.

Again, he nodded. "It'll take some getting used to, but it's a great feeling."

Alyssa smiled.

"Will you take me back?" Thomas asked. Her eyebrows rose.

"Will *I* take *you* back?"

"Yeah."

"Don't you think I should be asking you that question? After all, I'm the one who—"

He silenced her with a quick kiss. "Just answer my question. Will you take me back? Can we start over?"

"We've already started over, Thomas."

"You can call me Chris, you know."

"Why?" she smiled. "Your name is Thomas."

He smiled back and whispered reverently, "Thank you." He thought a minute, then turned his attention back to her. "Now will you answer my question?"

She threw her head back, and Thomas laughed with her. "Yes," she shouted.

"That's more like it."

Their laughter slowly died as they looked at one another.

"I love you," he said quietly. "And I won't ever hurt you again. I'll never let you doubt what I feel for you. I need you to believe that."

"I love you, too. And I don't have to believe it, I know it."

He smiled sadly. "Will you forgive me for believing Jeff?"

Alyssa sighed. "It happened years ago. I knew something was wrong. Now we know Jeff was behind everything."

"But Jeff didn't make the decision to leave you, I did."

She touched his cheek and outlined his lips with her fingertips. "Oh, Thomas, forget about it. I already have."

Once again, Thomas touched his lips to hers, but Alyssa reached up and grasped the back of his head, keeping him from pulling away. The slow caress of his touch burned bright within her.

"I think we should get these wet clothes off of you," she said when he stooped to pick her up.

"My thoughts exactly." He grinned. "But there is one other thing I need to ask you," he said, as her world turned horizontal.

"What's that?" She nuzzled her nose with his.

"Will you marry me?"

"But we're already—"

"Just," he grinned, cutting her off, "answer the question."

Alyssa laughed, loving how she could see remnants of Chris occasionally. He never had been one to beat around the bush. "Yes, Thomas. I will marry you. A hundred times over if you asked me to."

Walking upstairs with her, Thomas laid her gently on the bed and kissed her sweetly.

"See, I told you," he murmured against her ear.

"Told me what?"

"When you love someone? They're always a part of you. Not being with you these last few weeks killed me."

"I know the feeling."

"I always laughed at couples when they said they were meant to be together. After everything we've been through, I can't laugh anymore. Just think of all the obstacles we've jumped over. Like every path we took led us straight to each other."

Alyssa thought for a moment. "No more doubts, Thomas," she said simply.

Thomas smoothed her hair back from her face then traced his finger down her jaw.

He shook his head and whispered with a smile, "No more doubts."

About the Author

Stephanie Taylor is a homeschooling mom of three by day and a writer and business owner by night. She has a doctorate in Multitasking and can actually walk a tight rope while preparing dinner with one hand and typing her next novel with the other. You can find her online on Facebook and Twitter or at her publishing company, Clean Reads. www.cleanreads.com.

www.ingramcontent.com/pod-product-compliance
Lightning Source LLC
Chambersburg PA
CBHW030631120726
47904CB00006B/2111

* 9 781621 356646 *